The Case of the Case of
Mistaken Identity

Read all the Brixton Brother Mysteries:

The Case
of
the Case
of
Mistaken
Identity

BY
Mac Barnett

ILLUSTRATIONS BY
Adam Rex

SIMON & SCHUSTER BOOKS FOR YOUNG READERS
New York • London • Toronto • Sydney

SIMON & SCHUSTER BOOKS FOR YOUNG READERS
An imprint of Simon & Schuster Children's Publishing Division
1230 Avenue of the Americas, New York, New York 10020

This book is a work of fiction. Any references to historical events, real people, or real locales are used fictitiously. Other names, characters, places, and incidents are products of the author's imagination, and any resemblance to actual events or locales or persons, living or dead, is entirely coincidental.

Text copyright © 2009 by Mac Barnett
Illustrations copyright © 2009 by Adam Rex

All rights reserved, including the right of reproduction in whole or in part in any form.

SIMON & SCHUSTER BOOKS FOR YOUNG READERS is a trademark of Simon & Schuster, Inc.

For information about special discounts for bulk purchases, please contact Simon & Schuster Special Sales at 1-866-506-1949 or business@simonandschuster.com.

The Simon & Schuster Speakers Bureau can bring authors to your live event. For more information or to book an event, contact the Simon & Schuster Speakers Bureau at 1-866-248-3049 or visit our website at www.simonspeakers.com.

Also available in a Simon & Schuster Books for Young Readers hardcover edition

Book design by Lizzy Bromley

The text for this book is set in Souvenir.

The illustrations for this book were rendered digitally with a Wacom tablet and Photoshop CS3.

Manufactured in the United States of America

1014 OFF

First Simon & Schuster Books for Young Readers paperback edition May 2010

10

The Library of Congress has cataloged the hardcover edition as follows:
Barnett, Mac.
The case of the case of mistaken identity / Mac Barnett ; illustrated by Adam Rex.
p. cm.—(The Brixton Brothers)
Summary: When twelve-year-old Steve Brixton, a fan of Bailey Brothers detective novels, is mistaken for a real detective, he must elude librarians, police, and the mysterious Mr. E as he seeks a missing quilt containing coded information.
ISBN 978-1-4169-7815-2 (hardcover : alk . paper)
[1. Mistaken identity—Fiction. 2. Books and reading—Fiction. 3. Librarians—Fiction. 4. Police—Fiction. 5. Quilts—Fiction. 6. Mystery and detective stories. 7. Humorous stories.]
I. Rex, Adam, ill. II. Title.
PZ7.B26615Cas 2009
[Fic]—dc22
2008043305
ISBN 978-1-4169-7816-9 (pbk)
ISBN 978-1-4169-9769-6 (eBook)

For Shawn, old chum

The bookmobile steamed and roared in deadly pursuit!

Contents

viii   Contents

The Case of the Case of
Mistaken Identity

CHAPTER I

America's Favorite Supersleuths

STEVE BRIXTON, A.K.A. STEVE, was reading on his too-small bed. He was having trouble getting comfortable, and for a few good reasons. His feet were hanging off the edge. Bedsprings were poking his ribs. His sheets were full of cinnamon-graham-cracker crumbs. But the main reason Steve was uncomfortable was that he was lying on an old copy of the *Guinness Book of World Records*, which was 959 pages long, and which he had hidden under his mattress.

If for some reason you were looking under Steve's mattress and found the *Guinness Book of World Records*, you'd probably think it was just an ordinary book. That was the point. Open it up and you'd see that Steve had cut an identical rectangle out from the middle of every one of its pages. Then he had pasted the pages together. It had taken over two weeks to finish, and Steve had developed an allergic reaction to the paste, but it was worth it. When Steve was done, the book had a secret compartment. It wasn't just a book anymore. It was a top secret book-box. And inside that top secret book-box was Steve's top secret notebook. And that top secret notebook was where Steve recorded all sorts of notes and observations, including, on page one, a list of the Fifty-Nine Greatest Books of All Time.

First on his list was a shiny red book called *The Bailey Brothers' Detective Handbook*, written by MacArthur Bart. The handbook was packed with the Real Crime-Solving Tips and Tricks employed by Shawn and Kevin Bailey, a.k.a. America's Favorite Teenage Supersleuths, a.k.a. the Bailey Brothers, in their never-ending fight against goons and baddies and criminals and crime. The Bailey Brothers, of course, were the heroes of the best detective stories of all time, the Bailey Brothers Mysteries. And their handbook told you everything they knew: what to look for at a crime scene (shoe prints, tire marks, and fingerprints), the ways to crack a safe (rip jobs, punch jobs, and old man jobs), and where to hide a top secret notebook (in a top secret book-box). Basically, *The Bailey Brothers' Detective Handbook* told you how to do all the stuff that the Bailey Brothers were completely ace at.

The Bailey Brothers, of course, were the sons of world-famous detective Harris Bailey. They helped their dad solve his toughest cases, and they had all sorts of dangerous adventures, and these adventures were the subject of the fifty-eight shiny red volumes that made up the Bailey Brothers Mysteries, also written by MacArthur Bart. Numbers two through fifty-nine on Steve Brixton's list of the Fifty-Nine Greatest Books of All Time were taken up by the Bailey Brothers Mysteries.

Steve had already read all the Bailey Brothers books. Most of them he had read twice. A few he'd read three times. His favorite Bailey Brothers mystery was whichever one he was reading at the time. That meant that right now, as Steve lay on his lumpy bed, his favorite book was Bailey Brothers #13: *The Mystery of the Hidden Secret*. Steve was finishing up chapter seventeen, which at the moment was his favorite chapter, and which ended like this:

"Jumping jackals!" dark-haired Shawn exclaimed, pointing to the back wall of the dusty old parlor. "Look, Kevin! That bookcase looks newer than the rest!"

"General George Washington!" his blond older brother cried out. "I think you're right!" Kevin rubbed his chin and thought. "Hold on just a minute, Shawn. This mansion has been abandoned for years. Nobody lives here. So who would have built a new bookshelf?"

Shawn and Kevin grinned at each other. "The robbers!" they shouted in unison.

"Say, I'll bet this bookshelf covers a secret passageway that leads to their hideout," Shawn surmised.

"Which is where we'll find the suitcase full of stolen loot!" Kevin cried.

The two sleuths crossed over to the wall and stood in front of the suspicious bookcase. Shawn thought quietly for a few seconds.

"I know! Let's try to push the bookcase over," Shawn suggested.

"Hey, it can't be any harder than Coach Biltmore's tackling practice," joked athletic Kevin, who lettered in football and many other varsity sports.

"One, two, three, heave!" shouted Shawn. The boys threw their weight into the bookshelf, lifting with their legs to avoid back injuries. There was a loud crash as the bookshelf detached from the wall and toppled over. The dust cleared and revealed a long, dark hallway!

"I knew it!" whooped Shawn. "Let's go!"

"Not so fast, kids," said a strange voice. "You won't be recoverin' the loot that easy."

Shawn and Kevin whirled around to see a shifty-eyed man limping toward them, his scarred face visible in the moonlight through the window.

The man was holding a knife!

That was where the chapter ended, and when Carol Brixton, a.k.a. Steve's mom, called him downstairs to dinner.

CHAPTER II

An Exciting Case

THE BAILEY BROTHERS' DETECTIVE HANDBOOK tells you how to size up suspicious characters, which is useful if you're eating dinner with safecrackers, or cat burglars, or your mom's new boyfriend. Here's what the handbook says about identifying crooks:

> Hey, sleuths! Shawn and Kevin are always on the lookout for lawbreakers! You should keep your eyes peeled too. There are scoundrels everywhere! Spotting baddies is easy. They all look, dress, and act in a certain way! Take it from

the Bailey Brothers: There are really only three types of criminals, and once you've got their distinguishing features memorized, you'll be an unstoppable crime-solving machine!

TYPE 1: The Tough

Greasy hair
Scars on face
Stubble
Tattoos
Loud necktie
Cheap suit
Poorly concealed knife or gun
Limp

TYPE 2: The Ringleader

Red hair
Shifty eyes
Uses gel or pomade
Well-trimmed mustache
Turtleneck
Tall, slender build
Mysterious pinkie ring
Dressy trousers
Limp

TYPE 3: The Hermit
Long white hair
Wrinkly
Crazy gleam in eye
Missing teeth
Large beard
Uses an anchor as a weapon
Torn shorts
Limp

Steve's mom had a new boyfriend, a.k.a. Rick. Even though he'd never met Rick, Steve already knew he didn't like him. Rick might just be a dangerous criminal. Steve secretly hoped so.

When Steve came downstairs, Rick was standing in the kitchen with his hands clasped behind his back. His mom was there too, nervously stirring a pot of spaghetti. Steve strode into the room, looking hard at Rick but trying hard to look like he wasn't looking.

"I'm Rick," said Rick. "You must be Steven."

Rick was five feet ten inches tall.

"Steve," said Steve.

Rick had a blond mustache.

"I've heard a lot about you, Steve," Rick said.

Rick had no knife scars or prison tattoos. At least no *visible* ones.

"Great," said Steve, who never knew what to say when people told him they'd heard a lot about him.

It looked like Rick blow-dried his hair.

Rick didn't have a limp.

Rick was dressed in the tan uniform of an Ocean Park police officer.

And so even Steve had to admit that Rick didn't fit the description of a hardened criminal. Too bad.

For a few seconds nobody spoke.

"Dinner's ready!" said Steve's mom, a little too cheerfully.

Rick was off the hook. For now. There was always Bailey Brothers #24: *The Crooked Cop Caper*.

Rick may not have looked like a criminal, but he sure ate like a goon. When he sucked noodles off his fork, he sounded like a vacuum cleaner in need of repair.

"What do you like to do for fun, Steve?" Rick asked after slurping a seemingly endless noodle into his mouth.

"I don't know," Steve answered. "Stuff."

Rick raised his eyebrows.

"Steve's a big reader," Carol Brixton offered helpfully.

Great. Now Steve was going to have to talk to Rick about books.

"Oh, yeah?" said Rick. "What do you like reading?"

"The Bailey Brothers."

"Hey," said Rick, "those books were big when I was a kid. They're about spies, right?"

"Detectives." It took all Steve's willpower to keep his eyes from rolling. Only a doofus thought the Bailey Brothers were spies.

"Right. Detectives. The Bailey Brothers were those kids who were always riding around on motorbikes, saying 'gee whiz' and 'golly' while breaking up smuggling rings." Rick was smiling in a way Steve didn't like. "Well, let me tell you from experience, Steve. Real private detectives are nothing like those Bailey Brothers."

Steve clenched his teeth. He felt his neck heating up. The Bailey Brothers were real private detectives. This guy didn't know what he was talking about.

"Trust me," said Rick, tapping his badge. "I know what I'm talking about. In the real world, detectives don't use magnifying glasses. They don't race around in roadsters. There are no hidden passageways. Nope, private detectives spend most their time alone in their cars, eating french fries and spying on jealous men's wives."

Steve wished he could wallop Rick with a haymaker punch right to the kisser, just like Shawn Bailey would do. He looked at his mom for help. Unbelievable: His mom was smiling at Rick. She actually seemed interested in what this guy was saying.

"Yep," said Rick, "real detective work is done by the cops. Take the case I'm working on now, trying to catch this guy they call the Blackbird Robber."

"The Blackbird Robber?" said Steve's mom. "Sounds interesting, doesn't it, Steve?"

Steve had to admit it did sound interesting. Still, he wasn't going to say so.

"Yep. The Blackbird Robber. A jewel thief. This guy has been terrorizing all the rich old ladies in Ocean Park. Just last week he stole a ring from Mrs. Wertheimer, the woman who owns that mansion on the cliffs. This ring was worth fifty thousand dollars." Rick whistled. "He took it while she was on a drive up the coast. And nobody can figure out how." Rick leaned over his elbows and lowered his voice. "The whole place was locked up. Mrs. Wertheimer has the best burglar alarm money can buy. Motion sensors all over the house. Guard dogs so fierce you could catch rabies just from looking at them. I mean, this woman's got a serious jewel stash, and she's gone out of her way to make sure it stays safe, you know? But when the old lady got back home that night, the ring was missing from her bedroom. And get this: There were no broken windows, no open doors, and no fingerprints anywhere."

"My goodness!" said Steve's mom. Steve didn't say anything. But he was listening.

"Here's the weird thing," Rick said. "The thief didn't take anything else. This ring was sitting out on a dresser next to a bunch of necklaces, bracelets, fancy watches. But he only took the ring. Guess he's not too greedy." Rick chuckled.

Steve rocked back and forth in his chair. He could think better when he was moving.

"Why do they call him the Blackbird Robber?" Steve asked.

"That's the best part. Every place the thief hits, he leaves behind a calling card: a single black feather. This guy's so confident he's taunting us."

"How exciting!" said Steve's mom.

"Very exciting." Rick grinned. "I've been pulling up files on jewel thieves from all over the state, and I'm working some promising leads. See, Steve, that's what real detective work is all about: hard work and diligence." Rick emphasized his point by gracefully weaving a forkful of pasta through the air and slurping the noodles horribly. His mouth full of spaghetti, Rick said, "And don't worry. Rick Elliot always gets his man."

Steve looked right at Rick. "I'm not sure your thief is a man."

Rick stopped chewing. "A female robber, huh? Look, I've always believed women are equal"— Rick looked meaningfully at Carol—"but most jewel thieves are men. That's just a fact. I mean these guys steal jewelry—they don't wear it." Rick laughed at his own joke, and little pieces of spaghetti flew out of his mouth. "But sure, Steve, just for you: Rick Elliot always gets his man or woman."

Steve kept his eyes on Rick. "I'm not sure the thief is even a human."

Rick almost spit out a meatball.

CHAPTER III

Confrontation

THE DINING ROOM WAS SILENT. Carol Brixton looked nervous. "Steve, what are you saying?"

"I'm saying that I've solved the case. The Blackbird Robber is an actual black bird."

This time Rick *did* spit out a meatball.

Steve continued: "The black feather isn't a calling card. It's a clue. Crows love shiny things. They collect anything that sparkles and take it back to their nests. And they're very smart. A crow probably saw the ring through Mrs. Wertheimer's window and broke in to steal it. Check out the house: I'll bet you'll find a hole in the roof, or a tiny open window—something small enough for a bird to get through. That's why the thief just took the ring. It was the only thing light enough for a bird to carry." Steve smiled at his audience. "Case closed," he said. Finished, Steve leaned back in his chair and folded his arms across his chest.

Rick pulled at the end of his mustache, which was stained with tomato sauce. "Steve may be onto something there."

"Really?" Carol asked.

"Of course not!" Rick let out a harsh guffaw. "That's the craziest thing I've ever heard! Boy, you've got some imagination. A crow! Maybe he's teamed up with a monkey and a unicorn. I should call the zoo! A crow!" Rick began making crow noises, his squawking interrupted by snorts of laughter. It was hideous.

"Stop it!" Steve said. "Don't you know anything about crows?"

Rick kept laughing. Carol shook her head. "No need to be such a know-it-all, Steve. And don't lean back in your chair."

Steve put all four legs of his chair on the ground and slumped.

"A bird-brained criminal mastermind," said Rick. "That's real good, Steve. What do you want to be when you grow up? A guy who studies crows, one of those bird scientists, what do you call 'em—"

"Ornithologists." Steve said. "No, I don't want to be an ornithologist."

Rick tried to compose himself. "Well, what do you want to be? With an imagination like that, boy, you could go far."

Steve dipped a piece of bread in some marinara. There was no way he was going to tell Rick the truth. "I don't know yet," he said.

Rick twirled another forkful of spaghetti. "How old are you, Steve?"

"Twelve."

"Well," said Rick, preparing to slurp, "you've got plenty of time to decide."

But Rick was wrong. Steve didn't have time. In three days Steve Brixton would be the most famous private detective in the United States of America.

CHAPTER IV

An Unexpected Assignment

WHY MS. GILFEATHER WOULD ASSIGN an essay on a Friday was a mystery. Ms. Gilfeather, a.k.a. Steve's favorite teacher, was young and funny and had a ponytail, and she rode a bicycle with a basket, and she never gave homework on the weekends. Until today. Here it was, two forty-five p.m. on a sunny Friday afternoon, the smell of the Pacific Ocean blowing in through an open window, and Ms. Gilfeather was walking from desk to desk with a baseball cap full of essay topics.

"Reach in and grab a slip of paper," she announced to the class. "Your essay should be at least eight pages

Steve scrunched up his eyes and thrust his arm into the hat.

long. No playing with fonts. No swapping topics. Cite your sources. Papers are due Monday."

Eight pages. Due Monday. Impossible. Steve looked at Dana, his best friend.

"Due Monday?" Steve whispered.

Dana mouthed something Steve couldn't understand.

"What?" Steve asked.

"I believe he said, 'This sucks,'" said Ms. Gilfeather, coming up the row of desks and smiling sweetly. She held out the cap to Dana. "Lovely."

"I didn't know you could read lips, Ms. Gilfeather," said Dana, cherry-faced and embarrassed.

"There are a lot of things kids don't know about their teachers. Now pick a topic."

Dana plucked a piece of paper from the hat and examined it. "Detectives." He shrugged. "That's cool, I guess."

"What?" cried Steve. "That should be my topic."

"Luck of the draw." Ms. Gilfeather turned toward Steve. "Your turn, Young Mister Brixton. No peeking. Choose wisely."

Steve scrunched up his eyes, turned his head away, and thrust his arm toward the hat. He swirled the slips around with his hand. And then, when the moment felt absolutely perfect, he pinched a piece of paper between his thumb and index finger. Steve quickly unfolded it, eager to discover his topic.

His topic was early American needlework.

Dana leaned over and read Steve's paper, then started laughing.

"What?" Steve was aghast. "Wait, let me choose again."

"Sorry, Steve," said Ms. Gilfeather. "I said no swapping."

"But early American needlework?"

Ms. Gilfeather paused and winked at Steve. "Cheer up," she said. "Your topic may be more interesting than you think."

Doubtful.

"Please, Ms. Gilfeather? Couldn't I just write on another topic?"

But Ms. Gilfeather had already moved on. Steve slouched at his desk, his mouth hanging open. The bell rang. The class left. It was the weekend.

CHAPTER V

A Good Chum

THE BAILEY BROTHERS' DETECTIVE HANDBOOK says, "Every ace detective needs a good chum." When Steve first read this, it sounded like great advice, except he didn't know what a chum was. He'd had to ask his mom. Today, "chum" means raw meat used to attract sharks. Back when the Bailey Brothers solved their crimes, "chum" meant friend.

"Hey, chum," said Steve when he met Dana after school.

"Don't call me chum," said Dana, like he always did.

And just like they did every day, the pair walked

home with their hands in their pockets, down a road that ran along the ocean.

"I can't believe you got detectives," said Steve. "That should have been mine."

"I know," said Dana. "It doesn't seem fair."

"And now I have to write about needlepoint."

"Sorry, dude," said Dana. "I'd trade with you if we were allowed."

"No, you wouldn't," said Steve.

"You're right," said Dana.

The boys walked in silence.

"Want to come over and play video games?" Dana asked.

"I should go to the library," said Steve.

"Go tomorrow. It's not like anyone is going to be checking out books on knitting."

Dana had a point. Steve decided to go to the library on Saturday, delaying disaster for another day.

CHAPTER VI

Ruckus at the Library

IN THE BAILEY BROTHERS NOVELS, libraries are exciting and mysterious places, often located on the third floors of mansions owned by eccentric millionaires, many of whom are British. In Ocean Park the library was a squat building with peeling paint and orange couches. Dim light came from yellow tubes that buzzed in the ceiling. Nobody could tell whether the carpet was originally that horrible shade of grayish brown, or whether it had just gotten that way after thirty years without cleaning.

It wasn't all bad. The library had a pretty good collection of Bailey Brothers novels. And he liked the huge bronze sculpture of a book on the front lawn. Back when Steve was a little kid, he would climb on top of the sculpture and beat it like a drum. Still, it was safe to say that the Ocean Park Public Library was not the place you would want to spend a Saturday afternoon.

When he typed "early American needlework" into one of the library's ancient computers, only one entry came up:

TITLE:

An Illustrated History of American Quilting

AUTHOR:

J. J. Beckley

CALL NO.:

746.46 BECKLEY

Steve decided on the spot that *An Illustrated History of American Quilting* must be the most boring book ever written. Sighing, he picked up a stubby pencil and wrote down the call number. Steve sighed again, stood up, and went to find his book.

Walking down through the stacks, Steve searched for titles that sounded worse than the one he was looking for. He couldn't find one. Not *Footnotes and You*. Not *The Serious Skald's Guide to Medieval Icelandic Poetry*. Not even the *1993 Rotary Telephone Pricing Guide* was worse than *An Illustrated History of American Quilting*.

Finally, Steve found his aisle: NONFICTION SHELF #26B: 745–749.3. He scanned the books haphazardly, half hoping that the one he was looking for wasn't there. But then, on the bottom shelf, he saw it, the words "An Illustrated History of American Quilting" etched in its spine in gold. When Steve took the book off the shelf, a pillow of dust rose like genie smoke in front of his face. The book was big and heavy and bound in deep brown leather. Its pages were thick and yellowed. Its spine quietly cracked when Steve opened it. He was surprised to find himself excited. This looked like the kind of book that could contain magic spells or treasure maps or tales of long-lost lands.

But it didn't. Inside there was just a bunch of pictures of quilts.

Ms. Bundt was working the checkout desk and loading books onto a rolling cart. She was a round, prim, and kindly woman. Her face brightened when she saw Steve approach.

"Happy Saturday, Steve," she said.

Steve halfheartedly slapped his book on the checkout desk.

"Hello, Ms. Bundt."

Steve noticed Ms. Bundt was wearing a brooch shaped like a cat. This wasn't unusual—she was always wearing brooches shaped like cats—but this was a new one. Which meant she would want to talk about it.

"How do you like my new cat pin?" Ms. Bundt asked.

"Oh, it's really great," Steve said, pretending to be interested. The Bailey Brothers always say: It pays to be polite.

"It's Rumpelteazer, from *Old Possum's Book of Practical Cats*," she said.

"Cool," said Steve. He had no idea what she was talking about.

Ms. Bundt smiled and put on her glasses, which were hanging from a gold chain around her neck.

"Can I see your library card, Steve?" she asked.

Steve pulled out his Velcro wallet, removed a card, and handed it over. Ms. Bundt looked at it and frowned. She handed it back to Steve.

"I think you've given me the wrong card."

He had. It wasn't his library card. It was his Bailey Brothers detective's license:

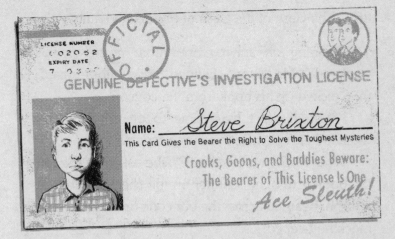

GENUINE DETECTIVE'S INVESTIGATION LICENSE

LICENSE NUMBER
002052
EXPIRY DATE
7 03

OFFICIAL

Name: *Steve Brixton*

This Card Gives the Bearer the Right to Solve the Toughest Mysteries

Crooks, Goons, and Baddies Beware:
The Bearer of This License Is One
Ace Sleuth!

The year before, Steve had sent away twelve cereal box tops plus $1.95 for shipping and handling to an address in Kentucky. Just twelve weeks later the license had come in the mail.

"Oops. Sorry, Ms. Bundt," he said. Steve put his detective's license back in his wallet and took out the right card.

"That was a pretty neat-looking detective's license, Steve," Ms. Bundt said cheerfully. "Maybe you could figure out who keeps putting gum underneath our tables." She laughed.

"It's probably Mr. Robbins," Steve said. "The gum's purple, right? He's the only guy I've ever seen chew grape gum."

Ms. Bundt looked startled. "Wow. I'll have to talk to him next time I see him."

Steve nodded matter-of-factly.

"Planning on solving any more mysteries this weekend?" Ms. Bundt scanned Steve's library card, then picked up his book from the counter.

"I wish. I don't have time to do anything this weekend except write this dumb report."

"What's your report about?" she asked as she ran the book across the scanner on the checkout desk. A red light beamed across the bar code on its spine. The machine beeped.

That's when all the power went out.

Everything—every light, every computer, the vending machine by the front door—they all shut down at once. The oscillating fans on the ceiling stopped whirring. A single shaft of late afternoon sunlight trickled down from a skylight high above. For a few seconds everything was strangely quiet.

Then came the alarm. First, a deep whoop rumbled through the room, chased by a shrill chirping. A strobe light blinked madly. It was pandemonium. Steve looked at Ms. Bundt for help. She was gone. There was a crash, then the soft sound of glass hitting carpet. Steve looked up.

A shadowy figure had just broken through the skylight!

CHAPTER VII

The Dangerous Chase

STEVE DIDN'T NEED *The Bailey Brothers' Detective Handbook* to tell him what to do next. He ran for the exit.

Through the glass doors at the building's front, Steve saw the world outside. A bicycle wheeled lazily by, a breeze ruffled the American flag on the lawn, and a robin hopped about underneath a tree. Steve wanted to be out there, not in here.

His chest heaving, he lurched forward and put his hand against the front door. Just as he began to push, an ear-splitting squeal came from the street. Steve watched as a huge black truck leapt up on the sidewalk and came spinning to a stop on the lawn. Immediately, six people, all in black, jumped out of the vehicle and ran up to the library's entrance. Steve stood frozen, panting, staring.

At the head of the group was its leader: a frighteningly large man with greasepaint smeared all over his face. He halted abruptly on the path that led to the library's entrance. The rest of the group snapped to attention behind him.

Steve and the man made eye contact. The leader pointed at Steve and made a series of elaborate hand gestures to the team standing behind him.

They're looking for me, thought Steve. *Why would they be looking for me?*

Steve remembered he owed $3.45 in overdue fines. They were really getting serious.

Without thinking, Steve pivoted and sprinted back into the library. Behind him he heard the library doors swing open and then booted feet tramping on the floor.

Steve ran back into the stacks and over to the library's west wall, which was lined with six tall windows. He stopped a few feet in front of the first one, looking for a way to open it. It was a single panel of glass, twice as tall as Steve and sealed shut. Steve stood and thought. There was no way out.

Then, without warning, a dark blur outside came hurtling toward the window. The glass shattered, and a man in a black jumpsuit somersaulted across the carpet. He landed in a tight crouch and looked at Steve. Steve ran.

As Steve ran past the second window, another man came crashing through it. The same thing happened at the third, fourth, fifth, and sixth—it was as if Steve were triggering the chaos. Steve did some quick figuring: Six through the door and six through the windows plus one through the skylight made thirteen people chasing him. He cut away from the windows and ran to the center of the library. The place was swarming with them, whoever they were.

"There he is! Get him!"

"No! He could be dangerous."

"Cover the exits! Make sure he can't get out."

He was trapped. Steve remembered a video he had seen in science class about the African savannah: a pride of lions had surrounded a wildebeest. He could see the terrified animal's heart pounding, its lungs expanding and contracting underneath its skin. Steve remembered the animal's frightened eyes; he saw the moment the wildebeest had given up. Right now Steve felt like a wildebeest.

Wildebeests get eaten.

But what could he do?

What would Shawn and Kevin Bailey do?

Hide.

Steve spun to his right and disappeared into the stacks. When he got to the end of the aisle, he made a quick left, ran down past three more rows, and turned down another one. Steve swung his backpack off his shoulders, unzipped it, and pulled out *The Bailey Brothers' Detective Handbook*. His fingers flipped to the section called "Hiding Places." He read as fast as he could:

> Sometimes situations get seriously sticky, and sleuths need to get out of sight. Shawn and Kevin Bailey know all the best hiding places! You can hide in or behind:
> —Grandfather clocks!
> —Today's newspaper!
> —Hide-A-Beds!
> —Duck hides!
> —Mailboxes!
> —Hedge mazes!
> —Sea caves!
> —Yachts!
> —Secret tunnels!

—Sewer grates!
—Airplane propellers
   (only when not in use)!
—Mexico!
If all else fails, get above a person's eye
level. You'll be much harder to find!

Steve looked around. There weren't any grand-
father clocks or sea caves. Too bad. He'd have to find
somewhere to climb.

Halfway down the aisle stood a library cart on
wheels. Steve hurried over to it and clambered on top.
The cart wobbled, and for a second Steve thought
he would fall. He steadied himself and picked out a
section of books on the top shelf. Steve had a plan.

Just then a deep voice filled the room. "All right,
ladies and gentlemen. Our target is trapped. We'll run
a sweep of the building, section by section. Today,
the Dewey decimal system is your best friend. Alvarez,
your squad takes Philosophy, Religion, and Social
Sciences. Kovner, your team is on Languages through
Technology. I'll take care of the Arts, Literature, and
History. Happy browsing."

There wasn't much time. As quickly and quietly as
he could, Steve took a few books at a time from the top
shelf and placed them neatly on an empty shelf below.

Steve could feel his lungs squished against his ribs. . . .

When he had cleared four feet ten inches of space, he climbed up and lay flat on his back.

Steve tried to stay perfectly still. It was tough. His belly heaved with every breath he took. His brain swirled. It felt like a thousand tiny fireflies were swarming in his skull, blinking off and on, urging him to run. But he had to stay calm. Steve counted to himself. One . . . two . . . three . . .

When he got up to three hundred seventeen, he heard footsteps. Steve held his breath and turned his head so he could see. It was the team leader, the one with greasepaint on his face. Slowly the huge man stepped forward, scanning left and right. Steve lay motionless. He could feel his lungs squishing up against his ribs.

The man continued down the aisle until he was just next to Steve. Then he stopped. Steve looked down onto the top of the man's head. He was so close that Steve could smell his shampoo. It smelled like peaches.

The man was staring right at the books Steve had moved.

His forehead wrinkled.

He scratched his nose.

Then, quietly, almost silently, the man whispered, "What's Plato doing in Native American Literature?"

Suddenly his eyes lit up, and he tilted his head toward the top shelf.

Steve's hiding place was blown!

In one fluid motion Steve swung off the top shelf and leapt onto the library cart. It was positively amazing: He didn't know he had ace moves like that. But before he could congratulate himself, the cart went flying from underneath his feet. Steve hit the floor face first. His nose was pressed into the brown carpet. It definitely had never been cleaned.

Dazed, Steve scrambled to his feet and spun around, throwing his fists in front of himself.

He was ready to fight, even if he had never thrown a punch before, even if his first opponent was almost seven feet tall.

But there was no need. His pursuer was slumped over the library cart, groaning. The cart must have rolled right into him! Elated, Steve made a run for it. Then he stopped, thought for a second, and doubled back to the cart.

"Sorry, buddy," he said as he gingerly pushed the man in black off the cart. The man murmured incoherently and curled up on the floor.

Steve crouched low and, using the library cart for cover, slowly wheeled his way to the back of the building. He paused by the dictionaries and checked out his surroundings. More books. A drinking fountain. A poster showing a guy slam-dunking a basketball with one hand and holding a book in the other, urging kids to READ! *Weird*, thought Steve. *How can he even see the hoop?*

Beside the poster was a door marked EXIT.

That was it. His only chance at escape. But bold black letters were painted on the door: EMERGENCY EXIT ONLY. ALARM WILL SOUND. Steve hesitated, considering whether people being chased through a library technically qualified as an emergency.

Suddenly, a shout broke the silence.

"I see him! Behind that library cart. Over by the fire door!"

Oh no.

"Take out your weapons!"

Weapons?

"Shoot to wound!"

This qualified as an emergency. Steve sprinted toward the door. He heard shouts from around the room.

"Fire!"

Gunfire erupted in the reference section. Steve crossed his fingers, clenched his jaw, and kept running.

"Don't let him get away!"

He pushed the door open. Immediately, another alarm pierced the room as sprinklers began spraying water from the ceiling.

"We've got water!" came a shout. "Suspend pursuit! Get those books under cover!"

Weird, Steve thought, then ran out the door. He was outside. He was free. Steve stood at the bottom of a flight of steps that would take him up to the street. The late afternoon sky was red, and the ocean breeze felt cool on his face. Steve leapt up the stairs two at a time.

When he got to the top, he saw a man.

The man had a gun.

The gun was pointed at Steve.

CHAPTER VIII

The Man Called Mackintosh

THE SHORTEST CHAPTER IN *The Bailey Brothers' Detective Handbook* is called "What to Do When a Man Is Pointing a Gun in Your Face." It's only four words long: "Do whatever he says."

"Hello, Steven," said the man with the gun.

"Steve," said Steve.

The man smiled. "Steven, my name is Mackintosh. Would you mind stepping inside my car?"

The man called Mackintosh opened the door of a black limousine that was parked just behind him. Standing there smiling in his black suit, he looked just like a butler—except for the gun.

Steve knew he should never get into a stranger's car, but he looked at the gun and realized he didn't have much choice. So he sighed, slumped his shoulders, and climbed into the back of the limo. Mackintosh got in behind him and closed the door.

Mackintosh took a seat across from Steve and put the gun in his suit jacket. To Mackintosh's right was a console lined with buttons. He pressed one, and Steve heard the doors lock with a dull thud.

Steve looked around. There was a small refrigerator in the back of the car. Mackintosh opened it, removed a water bottle, twisted off its cap, and took a long sip. He held the bottle with just four fingers, keeping his pinkie extended.

Steve was thirsty after all that running. "Can I have a water?" he asked.

"No," said Mackintosh. He took another sip. There was a gold ring on his little finger. "You have a lot of explaining to do, Steven Brixton."

This was insane.

"I have a lot of explaining to do?" Steve said. "Just who do you think you are?"

"I'm a Librarian."

That was not the answer Steve was expecting.

"And who were all those people back there?"

"Also Librarians."

Steve thought back to the dark figures somersaulting through windows and shooting guns. They sure didn't seem like librarians.

"Are you joking?"

"Oh, there's no joke," said Mackintosh. "Of that I assure you. You see, Steven, Librarians are the most elite, best trained secret force in the United States of America. Probably in the world."

"No way."

"Yes way."

"What about the FBI?"

"Featherweights."

"The CIA?"

Mackintosh snorted. "Don't make me laugh. Those guys can't even dunk a basketball and read a book at the same time. Every Librarian is a highly trained agent. An expert in intelligence, counterintelligence, Boolean searching, and hand-to-hand combat."

"Every Librarian? What about Ms. Bundt? She's just an old lady."

Mackintosh gave Steve a severe look. "Before Ms. Bundt worked the reference desk in Ocean Park, she was undercover at Biblioteca Nacional de Nicaragua. Central America. She got into some pretty heavy stuff down there. They call her *la Gata de la Muerte*."

Steve didn't even pretend to know what that meant.

This was a lot to take in.

"I thought Librarians just loaned people books for free," Steve said.

Mackintosh winced. "*Just* loaned people books? Listen, Steven: Librarians are the guardians of knowledge. And yes, we make sure knowledge is available, gratis, to everyone. 'Just loaning them books,' as you so crudely put it, is an important job." He paused and looked right at Steve. "But it's not the reason we're proficient in seven different kinds of martial arts."

Steve shifted in his seat.

"You see, Steven, some information is so secret that only a highly trained secret-keeper can keep it. United States Librarians make sure America's secrets don't fall in front of the wrong eyes. Trust me, Steven: Librarians are just about the only thing holding this country together."

Steve thought for a second before speaking. "I don't believe you."

Mackintosh leaned back in his seat and folded his hands across his lap. "Steven, have you ever wondered why it costs so much to replace a library book when you lose one?"

Steve had wondered about that. A lot, actually. Last

year he had lost a copy of Bailey Brothers #33: *The Case of the Missing Briefcase*, and he'd had to pay thirty-five dollars. It had totally wiped out his savings. He'd had to use all his birthday money plus the secret roll of quarters he'd had stashed in the battery compartment of an old flashlight. He even had to break open his old piggy bank, which, embarrassingly, was shaped like a cartoon puppy. But it's upsetting to take a hammer to a cartoon puppy's head, no matter how old you are, and to this day Steve felt bad about it.

"Yeah, what's the deal with that?" he asked.

"It's because they're filled with top secret information. Microfilms. Microfiche. Microbooks. And then there are the secret codes."

"Codes?" asked Steve. Steve loved codes.

"I thought you might be interested," said Mackintosh slyly. "Detectives love codes. Every book published in the United States is given a number by the Headquarters, a.k.a. the Library of Congress. These numbers hold encoded information for operatives at our various branches. Let me give you an example."

Mackintosh slid an alligator-skin attaché case out from under his seat. He unfastened a pair of gold clasps and pulled out a neon green book. Multiple bookmarks poked out from its pages. Steve leaned forward to get a better look. The cover showed a man standing on his head next to a title that was written to resemble graffiti: *Slide Slides and Body Glides: A Beginner's Guide to the Funky, Fresh Art of Break Dancing*.

Mackintosh opened the book to its copyright page and ran the well-manicured nail of his index finger along a row of numbers and letters: P6.A8S.C7BS2.Z51 SF.

"It's a cipher," said Mackintosh. "Code for 'Mouse Linebacker.'"

"Mouse Linebacker?" asked Steve.

"Quiet like a mouse, strong like a linebacker. Operation Mouse Linebacker was a Library program in East Berlin. And though few people know it, Mouse Linebacker was directly responsible for the fall of the Berlin Wall."

"East Berlin?" asked Steve. "That was a long time ago."

"It's an old book," said Mackintosh sheepishly.

"Then why is it in your briefcase?"

Mackintosh said nothing. Instead he quickly gulped down a mouthful of water.

"Are you learning to break-dance?"

"This is my interrogation," snapped Mackintosh. His tone was harsh, but his cheeks were pink. "And we're talking about codes."

"Right," said Steve. "Does every book have a code?"

"Absolutely. Of course, they employ a number of different ciphers. The one used here is one of the most common. Try it out on one of your own books if you don't believe me."

Steve shook his head. "I'm not sure what to believe. How can Librarians be the most powerful secret agency in the world?"

"Think about it, Steven. There's a library in every town in America. We're everywhere."

He had a point.

"There's just one thing I don't understand," said Steve. "If you Librarians are so secretive, why are you telling me all this?" Steve thought for a second. "Actually, there are two things I don't understand. Why were all those Librarians shooting at me?" At that point Steve thought of seventeen more things he didn't understand, but he kept his mouth shut. He didn't want to sound like a chump.

Suddenly the car door opened. Ms. Bundt stepped into the limousine and took a seat next to Mackintosh. The late afternoon sun glinted angrily off her cat brooch.

"I can answer your questions, Steve," she said. "We're telling you all this so you know we're the good guys." Steve breathed a sigh of relief. "We were shooting at you because you're the bad guy."

CHAPTER IX

An Astounding Story

NOW STEVE REALLY COULD HAVE USED that bottle of water. All the spit in his mouth had dried up.

"Look," Steve said, "I know I owe you Librarians some money for overdue fines." Steve pulled out his wallet. His hand was shaking. "I have five bucks here, so if you could give me some change, that would be—"

"We appreciate the gesture, Steven," said Mackintosh, pocketing Steve's five-dollar bill. "But I'm afraid this isn't about your library fines."

"Then what is this about?" Steve asked, watching his money disappear.

Ms. Bundt's eyes narrowed. "Treason."

"Treason?"

"You sound surprised, Steve," she said. "But then again, you must get a lot of surprises in your line of work."

Steve thought he must have misheard. "My line of work?"

"As a private detective," said Ms. Bundt.

Steve's brain swooned. He was speechless.

"Come now, Steve. There's no reason to play dumb." She nodded to Steve's wallet, which was still in his hand. "I saw your detective's license in the library, remember?"

Steve whipped out his Bailey Brothers detective's license. "This? Are you serious? This came in the mail when I—"

Mackintosh waved his hand in the air. "We don't want to hear a bunch of stories from your days in detective academy, Steven. The point is that you're licensed."

"But I'm a twelve-year-old kid."

"The perfect cover," said Ms. Bundt.

"This is crazy."

"Enough with the games, Steven." said Mackintosh. "We need to know about the man you're working for. Tell us about Mr. E."

"Who?"

"Your employer. Mr. E." said Mackintosh.

"Who is he?" asked Ms. Bundt.

Steve knew that Mackintosh and Ms. Bundt were speaking English, but nothing they were saying made any sense.

He tried smiling. "Look, there's obviously been a terrible mistake," Steve said.

"It's okay, Steve. Tell us about Mr. E." Ms. Bundt reached into her handbag and produced the library's copy of *An Illustrated History of American Quilting*. "Tell us about the man who had you check out this book."

Steve's head jerked back like he had taken a punch.

"I didn't check that book out for a man. I checked it out for social studies."

Ms. Bundt sighed. "You're making this harder than it needs to be, Steve. Stop protecting your client—he doesn't deserve it."

"What are you talking about?"

Mackintosh leaned forward. "Steven, if you won't tell us about Mr. E., maybe we can tell you a thing or two about him that you don't know."

"I'm sure you could," said Steve, "since I've never heard of him before in my life."

The Librarians were not amused.

"We don't know much about him," said Ms. Bundt. "We don't know who he is, where he lives, or what he looks like. We do know this: Mr. E. is a salesman. And he sells America's secrets."

"Sells them?" Steve asked. "To who?"

Ms. Bundt paused. The muscles in her neck tightened.

"*Whom*, Steve."

"What?"

"To whom. To *whom* does he sell America's secrets."

"Oh. Okay. To whom?"

"To the highest bidder. China. Russia. Insane billionaires. Sometimes he even sells our secrets back to us."

"Okay . . . but what does this have to do with that book on quilting?"

Ms. Bundt squinted. "Mr. E. hasn't told you much, has he? Although few people know it, quilting is one of America's most important pastimes. Needlework is more interesting than most people think."

"Are you serious? You sound like my teacher, Ms. Gilfeather."

"Smart lady. You see, Steve"—she glanced at Mackintosh—"all of America's most important secrets—the really secret secrets—are embroidered on a quilt. It's called the Maguffin Quilt."

This was so unfunny, Steve had to laugh.

"A top secret quilt? That's ridiculous."

Ms. Bundt nodded. "Completely ridiculous. That's exactly why it works. Nobody cares about quilts, so nobody would ever expect a quilt to contain important information."

She had a point.

"Betsy Ross started the Maguffin Quilt in 1776. She embroidered secret messages from General Thomas Maguffin to General George Washington on a blanket. It got passed around the colonies right under the British soldiers' noses. After America won independence, George Washington put Librarians in charge of the quilt. Since then every major American secret has been embroidered on the quilt for safekeeping. How to break into Fort Knox, who shot President Kennedy, the secret recipe for Heinz ketchup—it's all on there. The only problem is that somehow Mr. E. found out about the quilt, and he's been trying to get it ever since."

"Well, where is it?" Steve asked.

Ms. Bundt and Mackintosh looked at their knees at exactly the same time.

"We don't know."

"You don't know?" Steve asked. "I thought you were in charge."

"We are. But the quilt is so secret that only one Librarian knows where it is at any given time. The last person to know its whereabouts was Agent Beckley."

"Was?" Steve asked.

"J. J. is dead," said Ms. Bundt. "Killed in the line of duty."

"Wait—J. J. Beckley?" said Steve. "The guy who wrote *An Illustrated History of American Quilting*?"

Ms. Bundt nodded. She still held the book in her hand. "He was also the head librarian here in Ocean Park for sixteen years."

"I remember him! He was the old guy, the one with a lisp!" Steve said. "The one who was always saying, 'Thilenth, pleathe!'"

Mackintosh looked angry. "Mr. Beckley bit off the tip of his tongue during a parachuting accident in Afghanistan. His speech impediment is no laughing matter, Steven."

"Okay," said Steve. "Sorry."

"J. J. was one of our finest agents," said Ms. Bundt softly.

"What happened to him?"

Ms. Bundt looked at her lap. "Last year Mr. E. found out that Beckley was here in Ocean Park. So one of his henchmen made a visit to Mr. Beckley as he was closing up the library. He tried to force Beckley to reveal the location of the quilt. But a Librarian never talks. The henchman got angry. By the time I arrived, it was too late. Mr. E.'s man was gone, and Beckley was in bad shape. I could see I didn't have much time, so I asked him where I could find the quilt. He said it was here, in Ocean Park. I asked where. He told me, 'Look in the book. Use a symbol.' Those were his last words."

Ms. Bundt fell silent. Mackintosh gently took the book from her hands and continued. "We knew he meant *An Illustrated History of American Quilting*—it was Beckley's pride and joy, the result of a life's study of quilting. Of course, Beckley's book is more than just the definitive study of a classic American craft. It's also the only clue we have as to the Maguffin Quilt's whereabouts. Page forty-seven has a list of common quilting symbols." Mackintosh opened up the book and showed it to Steve:

Rhode Island Cross

Hudson Cross

Trident, or Pitchfork

Compass Rose

Simple Starburst

Paisley

Alphabet Soup

Eye of Providence

Star Over Springfield

X Mark

Patch Patch

Susan

Steve studied the page. Mackintosh said, "One of these symbols must be the one Beckley referred to. But which one? There wasn't a Librarian in America who could figure it out. We were stumped. So we set a trap. If we couldn't use the book to find the quilt, we could at least use it to find Mr. E. We leaked Beckley's last words, making sure they would reach Mr. E.'s ears."

Mackintosh took the last sip from his water bottle. "We knew Mr. E. would send someone for the book. So we've been watching it. When you checked it out, you set off the alarm."

"You're our only lead, Steve," said Ms. Bundt. "We've already investigated everyone with a last name beginning with *E*. Nothing."

Steve raised his eyebrows. "Don't you think that's probably an alias?"

"What?" said Mackintosh.

"You know: Mr. E., *mystery* . . ."

Mackintosh smirked. "And you say you're not a detective."

Ms. Bundt settled her hands in her lap. "So what do you say, Steve? Now that you know the man you're working for is a maniac and a saboteur, a man who will stop at nothing to destroy this country, will you help us? You can bring him to justice. And maybe even help us find the quilt."

Steve shook his head. "Obviously, there's been a mix-up. A coincidence," said Steve.

"We'll double whatever Mr. E.'s paying you," Mackintosh offered.

"But I've never met a Mr. E."

"Come on, Steve," said Ms. Bundt. "We could use a detective like you."

"I'm not a detective! I told you: I'm a kid doing a report for school." Silence settled across the limo.

Ms. Bundt nodded. "Protecting your client even though he's a villain. Just like a private eye." A fierce gleam flashed in her eyes. "Very well. We must take him back to headquarters. We can hold him there till he talks."

Ms. Bundt waved her hand like she was swatting at a fly. "Mackintosh, tie him up."

CHAPTER X

Rope Tricks

IF YOU FIND YOURSELF being tied up with rope, *The Bailey Brothers' Detective Handbook* has some pretty good advice for you:

Shawn and Kevin Bailey are always getting kidnapped——it comes with the job! But anyone who's ever read a Bailey Brothers adventure knows that these two supersleuths have a great trick up their sleeves. Remember this exciting moment from Bailey Brothers #3: *The Clue of the Ghost Shrimp*?

As the ship's captain tied Shawn and Kevin up with the rope, the brothers flexed their muscles with all their might.

"That ought to hold you two snoops till we can get back to land."

The captain grinned like a madman and left the cabin. As soon as he was gone, Shawn and Kevin stopped flexing. The ropes were now too loose and fell to the ground!

"That salty old sea snake fell for the oldest trick in the book! The Old Flex-Your-Muscles-While-You're-Getting-Tied-Up Trick!" Kevin hollered. "Works every time!"

Mackintosh pulled a coil of rope from a black briefcase. Steve narrowed his eyes. *Time for the Old Flex-Your-Muscles-While-You're-Getting-Tied-Up Trick*, he thought to himself. When Steve felt the rope against his arms, he clenched his fists, held his breath, and flexed with all his might.

Mackintosh wound the rope around Steve's top half. The rope was tight and chafed his arms. Steve kept flexing.

"Are you all right, Steve?" asked Ms. Bundt.

"Fine," said Steve, straining. His voice sounded like air escaping from a balloon.

"We're going to secure and reopen the library. We'll be back soon," said Ms. Bundt.

"Don't move." Mackintosh chuckled.

"Very funny," squeaked Steve.

Ms. Bundt stared at Steve. His face was getting bluish. "Are you sure you're okay?" she asked.

"Fine. Totally fine," he said.

Mackintosh opened the car door and stepped outside, followed by Ms. Bundt. As soon as the limo door closed, Steve exhaled and relaxed his muscles.

The ropes were still tight.

They did not fall to the floor.

For the first time it occurred to Steve that Shawn and Kevin Bailey had considerably bigger muscles than he did.

The Old Flex-Your-Muscles-While-You're-Getting-Tied-Up Trick did not work every time.

Panicked, Steve looked around the back of the limo for a knife, a jagged edge, anything he could use to cut the rope.

Nothing.

There wasn't much time. Then he noticed the console of buttons Mackintosh had used to lock the door.

Escaping might be easier than he'd thought.

Steve sidled awkwardly over to the buttons and peered down at them. Only one was marked. It had a white picture of a lock. Eureka! He brought his head down to the console and squashed his nose against the button. Nothing happened.

Escaping might be harder than he'd thought.

Frantically, Steve pressed another button with his nose. He was startled by a loud and brassy noise. An alarm! But soon the blaring was joined by drums and an electric keyboard. Smooth jazz. Smooth jazz was the worst.

But there was no time to turn off the radio. Steve moved his head to the right and hit another button. All along the walls of the car, panels lit up in delicate shades of pink, purple, and orange. Steve shook his head and tried another button.

There was a sharp hiss as smoke came through the car's vents and filled the backseat. *Poison gas*, thought Steve. Not good. He shut his eyes tight and took a deep breath. Steve knew it was only a matter of time till he would have to breathe in, and his lungs were already tired. He'd been holding his breath a lot today. Pressure built in Steve's chest. He waited till he couldn't stand it anymore, then waited five seconds longer. But it was no use. He needed air. He inhaled and opened his eyes to take in the last sight he would ever see. It looked like this was the end.

But there was no stinging sensation in Steve's throat, no burning in his eyes. In fact the smoke smelled like a haunted house.

Dry ice. Steve had turned on a fog machine.

Although Steve was happy to be alive, he was still trapped. He would have put his head in his hands if they hadn't been tied behind his back. Instead, he sat in the gently billowing haze, listening to smooth jazz and watching the colored lights play against the walls.

Fog.

Lights.

Twelve-speaker surround sound.

Mackintosh might work for the most powerful secret agency in the world, but he had apparently rented a prom limo. At least Steve was getting kidnapped in style.

There was one more button to try. Sighing, Steve brought his nose back down to the console and pressed it. There was a grinding sound as new light entered the car. Steve looked up. He had opened the sunroof.

Seconds later Steve's head popped out from the top of the car. There were no shadowy figures on the street. The coast was clear.

Steve ducked back into the limo. Although his hands were tied behind his back, he managed to pick up his backpack and loop one of the straps around his wrists. He also grabbed *An Illustrated History of American Quilting*. After this mess was cleared up, he'd still have to write that report. Now he was ready to make his exit.

It's not easy to climb out of a sunroof without using your arms. Hopping valiantly, Steve managed to slap his torso onto the roof of the limo before slipping back inside. He tried again, this time wriggling like mad. Steve looked like a salmon flopping around on the deck of a boat. It wasn't pretty, but it worked. Soon he had gotten his whole body up through the sunroof and on top of the car.

Now he had to get down. He rolled himself down the windshield, over the hood, and onto the pavement. It hurt.

Steve stumbled to his feet and collected himself. The Ocean Park police station was just a few blocks away. They'd help him there. Heck, he could talk to Rick, even though he was a gigantic doofus. Yes, it was time to go to the cops.

Crouching low, Steve picked his way along the sidewalk, hiding first behind a row of shrubs, then behind the sculpture of the book. Steve paused behind the bronze book, took a few deep breaths, then ran into the open. Ropes wrapped around the upper half of his body, he sprinted down the road like a sausage escaping from a butcher shop.

CHAPTER XI

Clumber's Mistake

THE SUN WAS SETTING as Steve walked through the front doors of the Ocean Park police station. The desk sergeant was deeply involved in a crossword puzzle. Judging from the number of blank boxes on the paper, crossword puzzles weren't the officer's forte.

Steve stood at the desk. "I'd like to report a kidnapping," Steve said.

The desk sergeant didn't even look up. "Who got kidnapped?" he asked.

"Me," said Steve.

The officer glanced up and did a double take when he saw the ropes around Steve's torso.

"Oh, man," said the officer. "Let's get these ropes off of you." He pulled a penknife out from a drawer and came around the desk to saw through Steve's binds. The ropes fell to the ground.

"Thanks." Steve rubbed his arms to get the blood flowing.

"Sure," said the desk sergeant. "Hold on a second." He picked up the phone and mumbled inaudibly into the receiver. Then he looked up at Steve. "What's your name, kid?"

"Steve Brixton," said Steve.

"Well, Steve, this situation is way above my pay grade. I think you'd better see the chief of police."

The desk sergeant led Steve through a door and back into the station. Things were quiet back there. The radio hummed softly. Two bored police officers sat with their feet up on desks. Steve recognized one of them.

"Hi, Rick." Steve waved.

Rick turned. His face was covered in tiny scratches, and his disheveled hair made it look like a bird had built a nest on his head. When Rick saw Steve, he just sat and glared. It seemed like Rick was having a bad day.

"Come on," said the desk sergeant. "The chief's up on the second floor."

Steve followed the sergeant up a flight of stairs and down a dingy hallway. At the end was a door marked CHIEF FRANK CLUMBER.

The officer knocked twice. "I've got Steve Brixton here to see you," he said.

The door opened. Chief Clumber was a large man, and his face was red and friendly. "Thanks for bringing him up, Sergeant Williams. You can go back to your crossword puzzle."

Sergeant Williams blushed and left. Chief Clumber winked at Steve. "He thinks I don't know what he does all day. Of course I know. I'm a cop."

Steve laughed politely.

"Don't just stand there in the door, Steve. Come in, come in."

Steve stepped into the office.

"Have a seat." The police chief pointed to a steel chair in front of his desk. Steve was wearing shorts, and the metal felt cold against his legs.

Chief Clumber scratched his right ear. "So. I hear you walked in here out of breath and all tied up in ropes. Very unusual. Unusual to say the least." Chief Clumber leaned back in his chair, revealing the full expanse of his massive belly. The buttons on his shirt deserved a Police Medal of Valor just for managing to stay fastened. Clumber smiled. "So, Steve, my question is this: What happened to you today?"

It was a good question, and like many good questions, it wasn't easy to answer. Steve tried to think. He placed *An Illustrated History of American Quilting* on Clumber's desk.

"It all started when I checked this book out from the library," Steve said.

Chief Clumber looked at the book and frowned. "Explain."

So Steve did. He told Chief Clumber about the alarm, the Librarians, and the chase, about Ms. Bundt, Mackintosh, and the detective's license, about Mr. E. and the Maguffin Quilt. As the story unfolded, Chief Clumber's frown grew bigger and bigger. When Steve finished, Clumber was silent. His face was now a deep and angry chartreuse. Steve realized how crazy he sounded. Chief Clumber probably thought he was playing a practical joke.

Finally, Clumber opened his mouth to speak.

"You're just a typical private detective, aren't you?"

Steve's mouth went agape. "What?" he asked.

"You heard me. You private eyes are all the same. Too good for us regular police—until you get into some real trouble, that is. Then you come crying to us for help." Chief Clumber snorted. "I should throw you out of my office right now, detective."

"But I'm not a detective!" Steve protested.

"You just said you were."

"No—I said that the Librarians mistook me for one. There's been a horrible misunderstanding."

Chief Clumber squinted. "What did you say your last name was?"

"Brixton."

"You're Carol Brixton's boy, right?"

"Um, yes," said Steve.

"So you're the one who solved the Blackbird Robber Case," said Clumber.

"Excuse me?" said Steve.

"Sergeant Elliot came in here this morning and told us about your crackpot theory. Everyone had a good laugh at the thought of a bird robbing old ladies. But I had a funny feeling. A hunch. So I sent him climbing trees to check out every nest in Ocean Park. Sure enough, he found the jewels in an elm by the harbor. Of course, the crow wasn't happy. Sergeant Elliot got scratched up pretty bad."

Steve was so elated he momentarily forgot his situation. "I knew it!" he cried. "I knew I was right."

Clumber shook his head in disgust. "You solve Ocean Park's toughest mystery over dinner and then tell me that you're not a detective. You must think I'm an idiot."

"But I'm just a kid. I don't know who these

Librarians are or who this Mr. E. is. You have to help me." For the first time all day Steve felt like he was going to cry.

Clumber rose slowly from his chair. "Look, I've never heard of these Librarians, and I've never heard of this Mr. E. guy either." He walked over to the door. "I'll go get a report and fill it out. But you can't expect me to give this case any priority. You made this mess; you've got to clean it up. Detective."

Steve wished people would stop calling him that.

Clumber shut the door to his office. Steve sat alone.

Steve had been waiting awhile when the fax machine in the corner started beeping. The machine buzzed and whirred as it slowly spat forth a piece of paper. From his chair Steve watched as, line by line, the fax printed out a photo. It was a picture of a human face. The face was strangely familiar—the hair, those eyes, that nose . . . oh, no. Steve was incredulous. He was staring at himself. It was his seventh-grade school picture, which had been taken at the beginning of the year, when he still had his retainer. He'd forgotten to take the retainer out, plus he had blinked when the flash went off, which is why this picture was the Worst Picture Ever Taken of Steve. He thought he had destroyed the copies, including all sixty-four wallet-sized prints.

Steve was overwhelmed by horrifying questions. Who had gotten hold of this photo? And why was it being faxed to a police station?

He was even more horrified when the words below his photo gave the answers.

WANTED

BY THE U.S. GOVERNMENT FOR TREASON

STEVE BRIXTON,
PRIVATE DETECTIVE

Warning: This individual is a highly trained detective and should be considered extremely dangerous.

ARREST ON SIGHT.

CHAPTER XII

A Daring Escape

THE LIBRARIANS! The fax must have come from them. In a flurry Steve ripped the paper from the fax machine and stuffed it in his mouth. (*The Bailey Brothers' Detective Handbook* says that eating secret messages is the best way to dispose of them. And even though the wanted poster wasn't exactly a secret message, Steve figured it would be better if Chief Clumber didn't see it.)

Steve chewed and chewed, mashing the paper into a wet pulp. Then he swallowed.

He gagged and almost threw up.

The fax machine started beeping again. Slowly,

steadily, the machine spat out another copy of the wanted poster.

Steve tore the paper out. His stomach gurgled threateningly. This time he ripped the sheet up and stuffed the shreds in his shorts pocket. The machine beeped again. And even though he knew what was coming, Steve was devastated when he saw his photo. He snatched up the piece of paper and crumpled it into a ball.

The machine started beeping.

Steve pounded every one of its buttons, trying to turn it off. But nothing Steve did could stop the fax from printing. Copy after copy of the wanted poster came spewing forth. Soon Steve's pockets were bulging with papers. By the time the tenth poster was printing, Steve was getting desperate. He swung his fist in the air and pounded the top of the machine as hard as he could.

The fax machine went quiet.

Then it started printing again.

In a wild rage Steve gathered the machine in his arms, yanked its cords from the wall, stumbled across the room, and flung it out an open window. Steve stuck his head outside and peered down to the ground below. Bits of metal were strewn across the lawn, shining silver in the moonlight. Sheets of white paper blew aimlessly across the grass. Everything was silent, beautifully silent.

Then Steve heard Chief Clumber's voice coming from an open window on the floor below.

"We got a lucky break here, boys. The detective's up in my office. Williams, Elliot, you come up with me. If he's as dangerous as the description says, I'll want some backup."

It appeared the Ocean Park police station was equipped with more than one fax machine.

There was no way Steve was going to let the cops turn him over to the Librarians. He leapt back from the window and surveyed the room, looking for something he could use to block the door. *The desk*, he thought. That should be big enough to keep the door closed. He hurried over to Clumber's metal desk and threw all his weight into it. It didn't move. Steve paused, caught his breath, and placed his shoulder against the edge of the desk. He heaved and strained. The desk still didn't move. But now his shoulder hurt.

Footsteps and muffled voices came from down the hallway. There was no time. Steve grabbed the book on quilting and stuffed it into his backpack, then ran over to the open window. He leapt up onto the sill. Sitting with his legs dangling fifteen feet above the ground, Steve pulled out *The Bailey Brothers'*

Detective Handbook. He flipped it open to a section called "Leaping from Tall Places" and began to read.

Jumping from high places isn't so bad— as long as you know how to fall! Shawn and Kevin Bailey are always leaping from old water towers or speeding trains. The key is rolling when you hit the ground!

Chief Clumber's voice was right outside the door. "All right, men, we go in on three."

Jumping from the second story of a police station didn't sound nearly as dangerous as jumping from a speeding train.

"One!"

Then again, the fax machine hadn't handled the fall very well.

"Two!"

Of course, fax machines don't know how to roll.

"Three!"

Steve jumped into the cool, dark night.

CHAPTER XIII

Manhunt!

ONE THING *The Bailey Brothers' Detectives Handbook* doesn't tell you is how fast you fall. Steve plunged downward and collapsed in a pile on the wet grass. A sharp pain shot through his left ankle.

Roll, Steve thought. Quietly groaning, he turned onto his belly, then over to his back again. His ankle didn't feel any better.

Clumber, Williams, and Rick appeared in the second-floor window.

"There he is!" said Clumber. "Get him!"

The three cops vanished from the window in unison.

Steve scrambled to his feet. His ankle gave. There was no way he could outrun the police. But Steve had an idea, and instead of running away from the police station, he ran back toward it. He lifted himself through an open window on the first floor. He was back inside, crouched on a cool tile floor. The room was dark, but the sweet smell of urinal cakes was unmistakable. He was in the men's room.

A few seconds later Clumber's voice came in from outside and echoed off the walls of the room. "Elliot, you check out the kid's house. Nichols, you take Main Street. I'll patrol the neighborhood."

"What about me?" asked a voice that sounded like Williams's.

"You watch the desk."

Steve heard three engines start up and fade away. He peeked out through the window. The front of the station was deserted. Steve gingerly lowered himself back onto the lawn and headed toward a place Clumber hadn't said to look: the beach.

At night Ocean Park Beach was completely deserted. Steve picked his way along the shore by moonlight, scrambling over rocks and splashing through tide pools. He wasn't going anywhere in particular, so after a mile or two he stopped going anywhere at all.

The sea was black and the sand was black, and the waves hitting the beach sounded like a librarian saying shush. Steve sat on the shore with his arms wrapped around his knees and wondered how his life had become such a mess.

The way he saw it, he had three big problems:

Big Problem #1: A bunch of trigger-happy Librarians thought he was a private detective working for a dangerous man.

Big Problem #2: The Ocean Park Police Department also thought he was a detective and was hunting him for treason.

Big Problem #3: He had a social studies report due Monday.

Steve grabbed a handful of sand and let the grains fall through his fingers. He wished that it would stay night forever, that he could sit by himself on the beach in the dark where nobody would find him.

He stood up, brushed the cold sand from his legs, and started walking. As his footsteps formed a great circle on the beach, Steve's brain unclouded. He began constructing a Big Solution.

If he found the quilt and unmasked Mr. E., that would get the Librarians off his case. Which would mean the cops would call off their manhunt. And hopefully the whole story would make for a great essay on needlework.

That was it: The only way to prove that he wasn't mixed up in this mess was to get mixed up in this mess. If he was going to show everyone that he wasn't a detective, he had to solve this case.

But first he needed to pick up the right tools. Steve walked away from the ocean, toward his house.

CHAPTER XIV

Under Surveillance

THE BUS WAS PARKED RIGHT IN FRONT of Steve's house: a great white thing decorated with rainbows and stars. A parade of brightly painted figures adorned the vehicle's side. There was a smiling butterfly, a bespectacled worm, and a teddy bear who held a book in one hand and a basketball in the other. All these creatures danced under the word BOOKMOBILE. In the orange glow of a streetlight the animals looked menacing. Steve stared at the bus. This was bad news. You could probably fit at least ten or fifteen Librarians in there. And they were watching Steve's front door.

Steve smiled. He knew another way into his house.

Crouching low, he climbed over his neighbors' fence and hustled to their backyard. From there he hopped another fence and landed on his back porch. Finally, Steve crawled in through his kitchen window. His mom always forgot to lock it.

Once Steve was inside, he stood still and listened. The house was small and its walls were thin, and Steve knew every noise in the night. He heard the dull buzzing of the refrigerator, the soft ticking of the wall clock in the living room, and the steady drip of the bathroom faucet. A note was sitting on the kitchen counter, illuminated by moonlight. Steve strained to read it:

Steve,
     The police say you are in trouble.
I am with Rick looking for you.
     If you're reading this, call my
cell phone. The police can help you.
               I love you.
                         Love,
                         Mom

Steve grabbed a pen from the top of the microwave and turned the paper over. He wrote:

Dear Mom,
   I won't be home this weekend
   because I'm wanted for treason
   and I have to clear my name.
   Also, I took the last Sprite
   from the fridge.
                  Love,
                    Steve

Steve put the note on the counter, took the last Sprite from the fridge, and tiptoed to the bottom of the stairs. Everything he did, he did quietly—the Librarians could have the place bugged.

Steve was very good at moving silently through his house. He was always sneaking around at home, practicing the Bailey Brothers' methods of stealthy sleuthing. Steve stood at the bottom of the stairs and looked up. The hall of the stairwell was lined with pictures of Steve: Steve graduating from preschool, Steve dressed up like Shawn Bailey for Halloween (no one had dressed up as Kevin), a sheep eating Steve's hair at a petting zoo. There was only one empty spot on the wall, where

Steve's seventh-grade school picture had hung until he took it down and destroyed it in the backyard.

Steve crept upstairs, avoiding the fourth, seventh, and twelfth steps. Those were the ones that creaked.

When he got to the top, he turned left and gently opened the door to his room. He reached under his pillow, pulled out a flashlight, and turned it on. *The Bailey Brothers' Detective Handbook* says every detective should have a working flashlight; you can use it to see in the dark and whack thugs in the gut.

Next, Steve opened his desk drawer and pulled out his magnifying glass. The glass was almost as big as Steve's palm, and its handle was made of brass. His mom had given it to him last Christmas. According to the handbook a magnifying glass is the most important tool a detective owns. Steve wasn't sure why. Probably just for looks. He slipped it in his pocket.

Finally, Steve slipped his hand under his mattress and felt around for the *Guinness Book of World Records*. He opened it up and took out his black notebook—that was the third thing every detective needed. Starting tonight he'd be filling his notebook with real clues and theories, not just lists of his favorite books.

Steve tossed the notebook and the flashlight

into his backpack. As an afterthought he threw the secret book-box in there too. Then he slipped out of his room.

Just as Steve was about to round the corner at the top of the stairs, he heard a noise. Not a loud noise. Worse. A very soft, very slight noise. Something was amiss. Steve peeked around the corner. In the reflection of one of the picture frames he saw a shadow move downstairs. Steve tensed. Someone was in his house.

Steve tiptoed into his room and gently shut the door. He slid his backpack off his shoulders, slowly unzipped the main compartment, and took out his flashlight and the handbook. He was going to have to exit through a second-floor window again, but this time he wasn't going to jump.

MAKING
YOUR OWN ROPE

Rope is useful! You can use it to pull loot up from a well, or to lower yourself from tall places. (If you jump from up high and forget to roll, you could end up hurting your ankle—or worse!) Here's a clever tip: When Shawn and Kevin don't have a rope, they make one by tying bedsheets together. The best knot for the job is a sheet knot, and it's a breeze to tie:

1. Twist the sheets and cross them.

2. Make a kitty.

3. Pull the ears and twist.

3. Under the mountain.

3. You will have a spare scrap of cloth—discard.

4. Take the ears and repeat steps 1-3. You're done!

Steve stripped the quilt and sheets from the bed and tied them together, trying to follow the instructions from the book. In a matter of minutes he had a rope long enough to reach the ground. He went over to his bedroom window, cracked it open, and tossed out the sheets. The white cloth cascaded down to the yard below. He tied the end of his quilt to a bedpost and gave it a tug to test its strength. It held. Perfect.

And that's when his bedroom door swung open. The light flipped on. It was Mackintosh.

"We meet again, Steven," he said.

"It's Steve," said Steve. "And I was just leaving."

Steve backed toward the window.

"I believe you have our book," Mackintosh whispered fiercely.

"I checked the book out," said Steve. "It's mine for twenty-one days."

"It's been recalled. Hand it over."

"I'd love to, but I'll need it to solve the case."

Mackintosh sneered. "I thought you weren't a detective."

"I'm not."

"But you're solving the case."

"Right."

"What are you doing back at home?"

"Grabbing my magnifying glass and some stuff."

"Grabbing your magnifying glass?"

"Yes."

"But you're not a detective?"

"No."

There was a pause. Mackintosh frowned. Steve bit his lip.

"Well, good night, Mackintosh," said Steve, finally. He gave a small salute, grabbed on to his quilt, and stepped backward out the window. Almost immediately, the knot on the bedpost slipped loose, and Steve plummeted to the ground.

CHAPTER XV

Midnight Pursuit

AFTER GOING TWELVE YEARS without ever once falling from a second-story window, Steve Brixton had done it twice in one night. His ankle throbbed. Again.

Since he was on his back, he could see Mackintosh poke his head out into the night and say something into a walkie-talkie. Steve got up. His bicycle was leaning against the fence. He hopped over to it, got on, and started pedaling.

Steve piloted his bike along the side of his house, dodging a garden hose, a shovel, and a rusty ironing board. He sped down his driveway. The second he turned into the street, the bookmobile's headlights flashed and its engine bellowed. The bus jumped into life and accelerated toward Steve. Bike and bookmobile were about to collide.

Steve braked hard, coming to a complete stop in the bookmobile's path. The bright lights grew closer. Steve shielded his eyes with his arm. He threw down his right foot, pointed his bike in the opposite direction, and pedaled as fast as he could. His tires left a trail of black rubber on the black asphalt.

Steve could hear the bookmobile steaming and roaring close behind. When he looked over his shoulder, he was blinded by the bus's high beams. The bike wobbled and almost tipped.

Steve didn't like the thought of being mowed down by a bookmobile. He jumped the curb and rode down the sidewalk. The bus pulled alongside him, and the two hurtled down the road.

Steve turned and looked up into the bookmobile. Hunched in the driver's seat was Ms. Bundt, her hands gripping a huge steering wheel. She turned and looked at Steve. Her hair was in a tight bun. Behind her bifocals, her eyes were set in a mask of pure determination.

He had to escape. He squeezed his brakes and swung his handlebars toward the bookmobile. The bike flew into the street, careened past the rear of the bus, and peeled across the road and down a narrow alley.

Steve's sneakers made rapid circles. The alley was dark. Steve turned wildly, avoiding potholes and piles of junk. Back on the street he heard the bus grinding and squealing. Suddenly the alley was illuminated by the bookmobile's high beams. Stray cats scattered away from the light, surprised. Steve pedaled.

The bus charged recklessly into the alley and slammed into a row of garbage cans. They went clattering across the pavement. Then there was a horrible shriek, like the sound of a thousand ghosts.

Over his shoulder Steve saw the bus. It was stuck, its metal sides grinding noisily against a brick wall. He rode on. Steve spilled out from the alley and onto a tree-lined street. He had to keep moving. Gradually, the sound of the bus shuddering and grinding faded in the distance. But Steve didn't stop. He sped through the back roads and side streets of Ocean Park. He rode for miles before he finally stopped to catch his breath, hiding behind a Dumpster in the parking lot of a Chinese restaurant. The place was deserted. Quiet. Foul-smelling.

Now was a good time to start solving a mystery.

Steve took his flashlight and notebook out of his backpack. He opened the book and began to write:

MYSTERY ONE:
WHO IS MR. E.?

SUSPECT	EVIDENCE
Mackintosh	Wanted me to give him the book; wears a pinkie ring
Rick	Jerk

His suspect list was a little thin. He turned to a blank page.

MYSTERY TWO:
WHERE IS THE QUILT?

CLUE #1:
Beckley said to look in the book and use a symbol.

CLUE #2:

Steve bit his fingernail. There was no Clue #2.

Steve pulled out Beckley's *Illustrated History of American Quilting* and opened it to page forty-seven. He copied the symbols down into his notebook. He scrambled them around, traced them upside down, and tried to read them backward. Nothing. Steve sighed.

Steve was stuck.

He needed a lead, but all he had was a Sprite. He held the can in his hand and looked at it. Steve wasn't supposed to have soda after nine p.m. He looked at his watch. It was almost four a.m. Suddenly Steve felt very tired.

CHAPTER XVI

A Clue!

WHEN STEVE GAVE HIS SECRET KNOCK on Dana's window, he noted gratefully that his best friend lived in a one-story house. A light flipped on inside, and Dana appeared on the other side of the glass, his eyes screwed shut.

"Hey, chum," said Steve.

"Don't call me chum," mumbled Dana. He scratched his head. "It's the middle of the night."

"Well, I've been running from Librarians who think I'm a private detective and breaking out of police stations. I need somewhere to hide out."

Dana was unfazed. "Come on in," he said. Steve climbed through the window. Dana threw a bunch of pillows on the floor and tossed Steve a blanket. They were both asleep in less than ninety seconds.

Late the next morning Steve was in Dana's kitchen, dipping Dana's mom's makeup brush in a tin of hot chocolate mix.

"Hey! You said you weren't going to ruin that brush," said Dana through a mouthful of toast.

"If I told you what I was going to do, I knew you wouldn't give it to me," Steve said without looking up.

"Well, what are you doing?" Dana asked.

"Dusting for fingerprints."

"Why?"

"Well, if Mr. E. didn't hire me to get the book, I figure maybe he went to look at it himself. But he was probably too smart to check it out. Which would mean his fingerprints would be on it."

"Do fingerprints even show up on paper?" asked Dana.

"Nope," said Steve. "But they'll show up on this." Steve used the makeup brush to gently apply cocoa powder to the shiny plastic the library had put over the book's cover.

"Well, well, well," he said to himself. The brown powder had revealed a bunch of swirly prints. Steve examined them with his magnifying glass. Through the glass the thumbprints looked pretty much the same, only bigger. He cut a piece of packaging tape and pressed it down on the book cover, then lifted it. A fingerprint was captured on the tape. Steve did this a few more times. Dana watched over Steve's shoulder.

"Okay," Steve said when he was finished. "We've got four different thumbprints here."

Four pieces of tape were laid out on a page of Steve's notebook. "One is mine. One will be Ms. Bundt's. Another one is Mackintosh's. And the last belongs to our first suspect."

Dana was impressed. "What do we do next?" he asked.

Steve looked at the *The Bailey Brothers' Detective Handbook*, which was sitting next to his plate, open to the section on fingerprint clues. Reading, he said, "Now we just match these prints against the ones I've got in my case files."

"Cool," said Dana. "Whose prints do you have in your case files?"

"My mom's. Mine. Yours."

An uncomfortable silence settled over the kitchen. Dana stared at Steve. "So unless Mr. E. is really me or your mom . . ."

"Take it easy on me," said Steve. "I'm still building up my files, okay?"

Steve hastily bit off a piece of a toast and paced around the kitchen.

"Okay. Here's what we do. Who has everybody's fingerprints?"

"The FBI?" said Dana.

"Yeah, but they're in Washington, D.C. Think closer."

"The police?"

"Right."

"Okay."

"So." Steve stopped pacing and looked at Dana. Dana shrugged.

Steve started walking again. "This afternoon we are going to sneak into the police station and break into their crime lab."

Dana groaned and put his head down on the kitchen counter. "How are we going to do that?" he asked.

"I've got a plan."

"Great."

Steve grabbed another piece of toast.

"First we head over to Barney's Costume Planet and rent a gorilla suit. You dress up like a gorilla—"

"Wait," said Dana. "Why do I have to dress up as a gorilla?"

"Because," Steve said, "you're the distraction. I'll be busy sleuthing."

Dana sighed.

"So you dress up like a gorilla and head down to the police station. You say you're a singing telegram for Rick Elliot. Say it's a congratulations for solving the Blackbird Robber mystery. From his mom." Steve laughed to himself.

"Then what?" Dana asked.

"You get all the police officers down to the booking room to hear your song."

"My song?"

"Yeah, you're a singing telegram. You sing and dance."

"And dance?"

"Of course. I'll need you to distract them for about fifteen minutes." Dana's eyes widened. "Meanwhile, I'll climb up onto the roof and crawl through the air conditioning ducts until I get into the crime lab."

"Steve, I don't even know how to dance," said Dana. Steve didn't hear him, or at least he pretended not to. He scratched his nose and did another lap.

"Actually, I may need a little longer. More like thirty minutes."

"What am I supposed to sing for thirty minutes?"

"I don't know. Maybe you'll need to do something else. Go around and have every police officer say something they appreciate about Rick." Steve doubted that would take thirty minutes, but he needed Dana to be quiet. "I'll access the fingerprint database. Then I'll run these fingerprints through the computer—I'll need to figure out how to do that, too. But I should have a match in less than an hour."

"An hour? How am I supposed to keep the cops busy for an hour?"

"I don't know. Bring donuts."

"Are you serious? Donuts? For cops? That's not a plan. That's a stereotype."

"No. Police officers really do love donuts."

Dana looked at Steve skeptically.

"I'm serious!" said Steve. "Ask any detective."

Dana sighed. Steve continued. "Once I have a match, we'll know who's been looking at this book. It could crack this case wide open." Steve tossed a bread crust on his plate. "That, my friend, is an ace plan."

Dana was looking in *An Illustrated History of American Quilting*. "I have a better plan," he said. "How about we check in with the guy who left his business card in the book?"

"What?" asked Steve.

Dana flipped the book upside down. A business card fluttered down to the tile.

Steve jumped over and snatched it off the floor. "A clue!" he said, and read the card:

Doug Grabes
Proprietor
The Red Herring Tavern
3434 Harborfront Drive
Ocean Park, CA

Dana smiled smugly. "Looks like we don't have to go to Barney's Costume Planet."

"That's what you think," said Steve. "The Red Herring is probably a hideout for all sorts of criminals. So we'll still need to do some costume shopping."

"Why?" Dana asked.

"Because tonight we're going undercover."

CHAPTER XVII

Down at the Docks

THAT NIGHT DANA TOLD HIS MOTHER he was spending the night at Steve's—it took some old-fashioned Bailey Brothers charm and politeness to convince her to let Dana go on a school night, but Steve pulled it off. The boys rode their bikes down to the Ocean Park docks. The docks had a reputation as a dirty, seedy place overrun by criminals and rats. That reputation was pretty much accurate.

As Steve and Dana weaved in and out among shipping crates and bumped down shabby roads, they began to wonder whether coming down here was a good idea. Finding their way was difficult. The few streetlights that worked at all flickered unpredictably, casting fearsome shadows on the ground.

They made their way to Harborfront Drive, a pretty name for an ugly road that curved along the coast. The night was mostly quiet and the road was mostly empty. Occasionally a set of headlights would waver in the distance, but no cars passed near. Offshore, fishing boats and container ships sulked in the fog.

"This place is creepy," Dana said, pedaling up to Steve.

Steve nodded bravely. "A lot of detective work gets done in nasty locations," he said, quoting a line from Bailey Brothers #7: *The Great Landfill Caper*. It was true: Shawn and Kevin Bailey were always hanging around dangerous places. That fact gave Steve some comfort. Still, he was pretty creeped out.

A couple miles of biking by warehouses and stockyards brought them to 3434 Harborfront Drive, a squalid building behind a parking lot full of cars. Steve and Dana pulled over and ducked behind a dented pickup truck. They peered over the truck's bed and surveyed the scene.

The Red Herring had been red once, but time and the salty air had peeled most of the paint away. Only blotches of red remained, and tonight it looked like the building had chicken pox. Steve and Dana couldn't see inside any of the windows from the parking lot. On the roof a neon sign alternated between the words THE RED HERRING and the outline of a fish. The fish looked more pink than red, and more like a bass than a herring. Loud men stumbled in and out of the entrance. A burly bouncer overwhelmed a tiny stool next to the door. He managed to look bored and angry with the same expression.

Steve ducked back down and unzipped his backpack. "Okay," said Steve, "I'm going in. I should be back in less than an hour."

"No way!" whispered Dana. "I'm not staying out here. This place freaks me out. Why can't I come with you?"

"Because," said Steve, pulling out some clothes, "they only had one sailor costume at Barney's Costume Planet. This is undercover work, remember?" He pulled a blue-and-white striped shirt over his head.

"Why can't I go undercover and you wait outside?"

"You really want to go in there? It's probably full of criminals. You're safer out here than you are in there."

"Fine," said Dana. "But what am I going to do while you're gone?"

"You've got to watch the bikes."

"Great. Like anyone is going to steal our bikes."

"Hey, bike theft is Ocean Park's number one crime." Steve applied some spirit gum to his upper lip, dabbed it till it was sticky, and applied a mustache.

Steve stood in front of Dana and held out his arms. He was wearing blue pants and a blue jacket, a striped shirt, a white hat, and a red neckerchief. On his face he sported a handlebar mustache and an eye patch. "Well, what do you think? Do I look like a sailor?"

Dana looked him over. "Definitely."

Steve turned toward the Red Herring. "If I'm not back in an hour, call the police."

"But the police think you're a criminal."

"Good point. Hopefully I'm back in an hour."

Steve walked out from behind the truck and up to the front door of the Red Herring. As he approached, the bouncer stood up and crossed his arms.

Steve remembered something from the Bailey Brothers books: Criminal hideouts always have secret passwords.

Steve did not know the secret password.

It was too late to turn back now.

CHAPTER XVIII

The Red Herring

THE BAILEY BROTHERS' DETECTIVE HANDBOOK has some very useful things to say about working undercover:

> Undercover work is fun—and dangerous! Don't blow your cover. Make sure you're familiar with colorful slang criminals use to communicate. For instance, did you know that thugs don't say "nose"? Instead they call that thing on your face a "beak"! And did you know that goons call machine guns "mowers" and bombs "Italian footballs"? Strange but true! And here's a useful

speaking tip: Crooks tend to drop the *g*'s off the ends of their words. A typical tough would say something like this:

"Didja hear 'bout Sam, that lob with the big beak? He was caught with a biscuit and now the judge is goin' to throw the book at him. Anyway, gimme my share of the do-re-mi and scram before I toss you an Italian football."

Steve got up to the entrance of the Red Herring. The bouncer looked down. "Good evening," he said.

Steve cleared his throat. "Look, buddy," Steve said in a voice that was much lower and meaner than his own, "I've been doin' a bit in the clinker. So I ain't been to this joint in a while. I gotta admit: I forgot the secret password."

Confusion spread across the bouncer's lumpy face. "There is no secret password," the bouncer replied.

"Of course there ain't," Steve said. He gave the bouncer a friendly pat on the arm and walked through the front door. He was in!

The inside of the Red Herring was shabby and dim and smelled like beards. The wallpaper peeled off the walls like it was trying to escape. At the back of the room a tough was wiping down the bar with a filthy rag. Bottles of all colors glistened on a shelf behind the bartender's head. Every table in the room was full. Unshaven men sat huddled in conversation or leaned back recklessly in their chairs.

The men stared at Steve when he entered the room. Conscious of his disguise, Steve examined the patrons' clothes. Everyone was dressed normally, wearing jeans or work pants, white tees or flannel shirts. *Yes!* Steve thought, catching his reflection in a gaudy mirror. He looked more like a sailor than anyone in the place.

Steve sauntered over to the bar and climbed onto a stool.

"Evenin', buster," Steve said.

"Hello." The bartender frowned. He looked like a gorilla in shirtsleeves. "What can I get you?"

"A glass of milk," said Steve. "On the rocks," he added.

The man looked at Steve for a second before turning around and opening a refrigerator. He pulled out a carton of milk and poured it into a tall glass filled with ice.

He set the milk on the bar. "Anything else?" he asked.

"A straw," said Steve.

Yes! Steve thought. *I look more like a sailor than anyone in this place!*

The man gave Steve a straw. Steve put it in the glass and took a long sip. The bartender watched.

"Say," Steve said casually. "Can you tell me where I can find Mr. Grabes?"

The bartender stiffened. "Mr. Grabes doesn't like visitors."

"Well I'd like to see him all the same," said Steve.

The bartender leaned forward. "Just who do you think you are?" he asked.

Steve looked down at his milk. His face flushed, and he starting sweating. "Don't get your beak all bent outta shape," he said. "I'm just a sailor."

"Pretty small for a sailor."

"That's why they call me Shorty," said Steve.

"Oh, yeah?" said the man. "What ship are you with, Shorty?"

Steve tried to think of an answer. Sweat poured down his nose. He could feel it loosening the adhesive on his mustache. And still he couldn't come up with the name of a ship. The only thing he could think of was Christopher Columbus.

"I'm on the crew of the *Santa Maria*," Steve said.

Steve's mustache fell off his face and plopped into his milk.

CHAPTER XIX

A Secret Unveiled!

THE BARTENDER EXHALED through his nose noisily. His right hand, still resting on the bar, closed into a fist. "We don't like your kind around here," he said.

"Look, I know I'm just a kid, but—"

"Not kids. Detectives."

Steve slumped. Not again.

"But I'm not a detective," he said.

"Oh, you're not?"

"No!"

"Let me get this straight. You're dressed up like a sailor, wearing a fake mustache, and snooping around my bar. Sounds like a detective to me. Scram."

"But—"

"Fine. I'll help you scram." The bartender leapt over the bar and grabbed Steve's arm. Together they walked to the front door, Steve shuffling a few steps behind the huge man. A few sailors looked up from their drinks to watch them.

The bartender shoved Steve through the exit and followed him outside. The bouncer glanced up—now his expression was simultaneously bored, angry, and curious.

"We got a detective here," said the bartender to the bouncer. "Wanted to go up to see Mr. Grabes. Make sure he doesn't come back inside."

The bouncer nodded. The bartender ducked back inside.

Steve rubbed his arms. It was cold.

Steve didn't smile, but he wanted to. The key to good sleuthing is good listening: The bartender had said that Steve wanted to go *up* to see Doug Grabes. That meant Grabes must be on the second floor. Steve grinned at the bouncer. The bouncer stared at Steve.

"Good night," Steve said cheerfully, and walked around to the back of the Red Herring.

The alley was lit by a flood lamp mounted to the back of the building. Steve smelled garbage and heard rats. He looked up. There were four windows on the second floor. All but one were dark. The flood lamp was about eight feet off the ground and two feet below an unlit, open window. If he could use the lamp as a foothold, he could climb into the building. From there he'd find his way to Grabes's office.

Steve scurried into the shadows of the alley and carefully picked up a steel trash can. He carried it over to the wall of the Red Herring and delicately set it down underneath the flood lamp. Slowly, Steve climbed onto the can. He stood up. There was a sharp pop as the lid dented under his weight. Steve froze and counted to thirty. Nobody came to check on the noise.

The flood lamp was now just below Steve's waist. Steadying himself against the wall of the building, he stepped gingerly onto the flood lamp. At first he put only a little weight on it, testing to see if the lamp would hold. It did.

Steve looked at the window. If he did this right, he could launch himself into the building in one movement. *Here we go*, he thought as he stepped off the trash can and pushed against the lamp.

The flood lamp immediately gave way, bending as if on a hinge, and Steve tumbled to the pavement. Steve closed his eyes in pain, but he opened them when he heard a low rumbling. Something had changed about the back of the Red Herring: There was a hole where there once had been a wall. The lamp had activated a secret passageway.

CHAPTER XX

Surprising a Suspect

STEVE TOOK OUT HIS FLASHLIGHT and pointed it toward the hole in the wall. The beam revealed a flight of steps that ran upward in a tight spiral. Taking the stairs looked easier than climbing the wall. Steve entered the passageway.

He was inside the walls of the Red Herring. As he circled upward, Steve could hear the low bass of music from the bar and water rushing through pipes. The air was warm and damp.

The stairs ran right into a dead end. Steve shone his flashlight around the wall until he found a small black button. He took a deep breath and pressed it with his index finger. The wall swung open, revealing a brightly illuminated room. A startled man sat at a desk, a white napkin tied around his neck. He had a fork in one hand and a knife in the other. A poached trout lay on a plate in front of him.

"Doug Grabes," said Steve.

The wall behind Grabes was covered with taxidermized fish mounted on wood plaques. The fish were strange and horrible-looking—black and huge with sharp teeth and bulbous protrusions. Steve hated fish. He hated the way they tasted and the way they smelled, but more than anything he hated the way they looked. The problem was in the eyes. There was no difference between the eye of a dead fish and the eye of a live one. Standing in the doorway, Steve felt the gaze not only of Doug Grabes, but of many dead fish. His stomach twisted. "Nice office."

"Why'd you take the secret passageway?" asked Grabes.

"What?" asked Steve.

"I've been waiting for you. You should have just told Ringo you were the detective sent by Mr. E."

Steve sunk. "You must be joking."

CHAPTER XXI

A Handsome Reward

DOUG GRABES WAS A NASTY, brutish, and short man. Tattoos of anchors and dragons ran up and down his thick arms. His head was bald, and his patchy beard did a poor job of hiding his scars.

"It's an honor," said Grabes. But he didn't sound like he meant it. "Come in." There was only one chair in the room, and Doug Grabes was in it. Steve leaned awkwardly against a filing cabinet.

Doug Grabes gave Steve a once-over as he stuffed a forkful of trout in his mouth. "What an outfit," he said dryly. "I thought detectives were supposed to be snappy dressers."

"How many times do I have to tell you people? I'm not a detective."

"You're not Steve Brixton?"

Steve was dumbstruck. "How do you know my name?"

Doug Grabes opened up his desk drawer and pulled out a copy of the wanted poster that had been faxed to the police station. "You're famous, Brixton," he said.

Steve swallowed hard. "How'd you get a hold of that?"

"I'm pretty good at getting a hold of things, Brixton. It's a specialty of mine."

"I imagine it would be." Steve paused dramatically. "Since you're Mr. E.!"

Doug Grabes started wheezing again. "Mr. E.! That's good, detective. You think if I was Mr. E. I'd be in a dump like this? No, I work for Mr. E. Just like you." He eyed Steve conspiratorially. "So, do you have the book?"

"Sure I do," said Steve.

"Good. Good. Then you've come to the right place."

Grabes ate the last piece of fish.

"If you're so good at getting a hold of things, why didn't you get the book yourself?" Steve asked.

Grabes took out a pipe and lit it with a silver lighter he kept on his desk. "You kidding me? Too dangerous. Librarians and me, we don't get along too hot. The way they were watching that thing, I was afraid to even slip my card in there. But Mr. E. told me to, and what Mr. E. says goes." He paused thoughtfully. "Anyway, my orders were to sit and wait for the book. When I saw this wanted poster, I knew Mr. E. had put a professional on the case."

"I'm not a professional," said Steve.

"Sure, sure," said Grabes. "You do it for the love. But the money's not bad, right?" He laughed and wheezed and coughed, all at the same time. "All right, enough chatting. Where's the book?"

Steve took off his backpack and pulled out *An Illustrated History of American Quilting*.

"Right here."

"Well, well, well," said Grabes, looking at the book the same way he'd looked at his trout. "Let me get your reward." Grabes rose from the desk and stood on his chair. He removed one of the mounted fish from the wall, revealing the door to a large steel safe. Grabes covered the dial with his hand so Steve couldn't see the combination. The door swung open. He pulled out four stacks of green bills and tossed them on his desk.

"How much is that?" Steve asked.

"That's forty thousand dollars."

Steve tried to whistle, but he didn't know how.

"So, do we have a deal?" Grabes asked.

Steve smiled. "Nope," he said.

Doug Grabes looked like he'd been punched in the stomach. "What?"

"If I'm going to give this book to Mr. E., I want to see him in person."

Doug Grabes guffawed. "Good luck!" He perched on the edge of his desk. "Look, I'm as close to Mr. E. as you're ever gonna get. Don't be an idiot, Steve. Give me the book and take the money."

"Sorry, Mr. Grabes. No deal." Steve put the book back in his backpack.

"I was hoping it wouldn't come to this," said Grabes. He pressed a button on his desk. "Ringo," he said, "get in here."

The door opened and the bartender filled the frame.

"Shake him down," said Doug Grabes.

Steve raised his fists in front of his face and looked up at Ringo. Ringo grinned down at Steve.

CHAPTER XXII

Fight!

THE BAILEY BROTHERS' DETECTIVE HANDBOOK tells you how to throw the Shawn Bailey haymaker punch, which is sure to knock out thugs, toughs, and thick-necked enforcers.

The Bailey Brothers aren't just ace detectives and terrific students—they're swell athletes, too! Between the two of them, Shawn and Kevin have lettered in practically every varsity sport. Shawn's a first-class boxer: His patented haymaker punch is the talk of Bridgeport's boxing rings—and the bane of all the town's criminals! You can throw one too. Here's how!

STEP ONE: THE WIND-UP

STEP TWO: THE PATH

STEP THREE: CONTACT!

Steve positioned his right fist about a foot from his ear. Ringo looked mildly intrigued. Steve brought his fist around in a clean, wide arc. Ringo was tall, so the punch landed with full force right under the bartender's ribs. It hurt—Steve. A sharp pain started at Steve's knuckles and shot up to his elbow. Steve winced. Ringo's expression didn't change.

The bartender sighed, stepped forward, and matter-of-factly hugged Steve under his right arm. Steve struggled but couldn't get out of Ringo's embrace. It was a little embarrassing.

With his left hand Ringo unzipped Steve's backpack and pulled out *An Illustrated History of American Quilting*. "Here it is, boss," he said, and tossed the book on Grabes's desk. Ringo relaxed his grip. Steve shook himself off.

"Nicely done, Ringo," said Grabes. He picked up the book and eagerly thumbed through it. But his smirk turned into a gape as he frantically flipped the pages. Steve hid a smile.

"Where's page forty-seven?" asked Grabes. "Beckley's list of symbols?"

"Oh, I tore that page out and put it somewhere safe," said Steve.

"What?" Grabes shrieked.

Steve felt Ringo move behind him. He ducked the

bartender's grip and lunged toward Grabes's desk. In a flash Steve snatched up Grabes's lighter and a stack of bills. He held the flame close to the money.

"Easy, Grabes," said Steve. "If this guy lays a hand on me, forty thousand dollars goes up in flames."

The room was still. Grabes fumed. Ringo glared. Steve backed out through the door, the money and the lighter in his hands.

As Steve moved down the hall, Grabes and Ringo cautiously followed. The three moved uneasily down the stairs, their eyes darting constantly.

Steve stepped into the main room of the Red Herring and climbed over the bar, never taking his eyes off his pursuers.

"Hey, everyone!" shouted Steve.

The bar grew silent.

Steve held the stack over his head. He peeled off the rubber band with his fingers. "Free money!"

Steve flung the bills into the air. They floated down like green confetti. The sailors and longshoremen leapt from their chairs and went scrambling around the room. Shouts erupted and punches flew as they grabbed at the money.

"Stop it!" said Grabes. "Ringo, grab that money!" Steve ducked into the moving mass of bodies.

Under cover of chaos Steve forced his way out

the front door and took off across the parking lot. He sprinted over to the pickup truck where Dana was waiting. Steve hoped nobody had stolen the bikes. They needed to make a quick getaway. He ducked behind the truck.

The bikes were still there.

Dana was missing.

CHAPTER XXIII

The Missing Chum

IT'S A WELL-KNOWN FACT that the chums of detectives are always getting kidnapped. For instance, Shawn and Kevin Bailey's best friend, Ernest Plumly, gets abducted in thirty-two of the fifty-nine Bailey Brothers adventures. Every time, the Bailey Brothers always come to the rescue.

Steve knew it was his responsibility to find his best chum. He hopped on his bike, rode down to an abandoned warehouse, and crouched behind a crate. He pulled out his black notebook and drew up a suspect list.

MYSTERY THREE:
WHO KIDNAPPED DANA?

SUSPECT	MOTIVE
Doug Grabes	Works for Mr. E.
Mr. E.	Wants the book (Grabes had wanted poster— is Mr. E. a Librarian?)
Rick	Jerk

At this point Steve was putting Rick on the list just to make it look longer. He'd start with Grabes. It looked like it was time for a stakeout. Steve rubbed his hands together, partly because he was excited and partly because it was chilly. This was going to be a long night.

Just then something blunt hit the back of Steve's head, and everything went black.

CHAPTER XXIV

Captured!

WHEN STEVE CAME TO, he couldn't tell whether the room was swaying or just his head. Although Steve's eyes were open, he couldn't see anything. There were no windows and no lights. The air had the warmth and smell of wet breath. He didn't know how long he'd been knocked out. He didn't know where he was. And the only person who knew he'd gone to the Red Herring had been kidnapped. He might as well have not even existed.

"Where am I?" Steve asked aloud in the dark, just to prove he was real.

"In a boat," said a voice right behind him. The voice sounded both familiar and irritated.

"Hey, chum!" Steve said excitedly.

"Don't call me chum," said Dana.

Steve tried to stand up and discovered that he was tied to a chair.

"I'm tied to a chair!" said Steve.

"I know," said Dana.

"Are you tied to a chair?" asked Steve.

"Yes."

Steve and Dana were bound together back-to-back, tied by ropes to a pair of wooden chairs. For a few seconds no one spoke.

"We need to find a way out of here," Steve said.

"We?" asked Dana. "You're the one with all the plans."

Dana was right. Steve started thinking. Then he had an idea.

"Help!" Steve screamed. He started stomping on the floor with his feet. The floor was metal, and the noise was tremendous. "Help us!" Steve screamed. Grudgingly, Dana joined in.

After a few minutes their voices were hoarse and their throats were burning. Steve and Dana screamed and pounded halfheartedly for a while longer, then gave up. The only sound in the room was the ringing in their ears.

Then something in the roof started squeaking. A

shaft of light entered the room from above. Someone had opened a hatch. High above, a square of swirling fog was framed like a painting on the ceiling. It was beautiful. That is, it was beautiful until Doug Grabes's ugly head entered the frame. The light from behind blotted out Grabes's features. He was just a hideous silhouette.

"I wondered how long you boys could keep up the noise." He looked at his wristwatch. "Five minutes. Very impressive. But let me ask you this: You're on a boat, and I'm the only other person on board. Now, who do you think is going to rescue you?"

Steve felt stupid, and his face flushed.

"You'll never get away with this, Grabes!" he said lamely.

"Oh, dear," said Grabes with a frown. "You detectives always say that. I've heard it probably a thousand times. And you know what? I always get away with it."

Steve felt even dumber.

"Look," said Grabes. "You want to get out of here. Fine. Just tell me where you've hidden Beckley's list of symbols, we'll head back to shore, and we can go our separate ways."

Steve was silent.

"No?" said Grabes. "Well, I'll give you some time

to reconsider. Tell you what: I'll be back in five hours."
He started to close the hatch.

"Wait!" Steve shouted. "The police knew I was going to the Red Herring, They'll be on our trail. It's only a matter of time before they show up with a fleet of Coast Guard cutters."

He was bluffing.

"You're bluffing," said Doug Grabes, and slammed the hatch shut.

Everything was dark again.

CHAPTER XXV

A Daring Plan

"WHO WAS THAT GUY?" ASKED DANA.

"He works for Mr. E.," Steve said glumly.

"He seemed angry."

"I lost him forty thousand dollars."

"Oh. Well, now what do we do?" Dana asked.

"Let's try chewing through the ropes," said Steve.

"Are you serious?" asked Dana.

Steve didn't reply because he had a thick braid of rope in his mouth, and he was sawing away. After a while his teeth stung and his jawbone ached. The rope was wet with spit, but other than that it was still solid.

"How's it going?" Dana asked.

"Not too bad," said Steve. He needed a new plan. "I need to move around. I think better when I'm moving."

"Well, that might be hard, seeing as we're tied to chairs," said Dana.

"We'll have to coordinate this," said Steve. "Stand on three. One."

"What?"

"Two."

Dana sighed.

"Three."

Steve and Dana stood up at the same time, their chairs' legs lifting a few inches off the ground. They were stuck in an awkward crouch, their backs arched and knees flexed. Holding this position was tough, and their leg and stomach muscles were burning.

"All right," said Steve. "Let's move."

Steve and Dana awkwardly coordinated their movements. Steve led; Dana followed. Together they scuttled around the room like a stunned crab. As Steve moved, he felt his mind unmuddy. He began to think the situation through. There was no way they could break through their ropes. But maybe . . .

"Dana," said Steve. "Let's shatter these chairs."

"How are we going to do that?"

"They're just made out of wood. If we slam them

against the wall a couple times, we should be able to break them."

It sounded pretty good.

In the darkness Steve and Dana waddled over to the wall, stopping when they felt the cool metal against their shoulders. Then they took three steps toward the middle of the room.

"All right," said Steve, "we've got about three feet to get our speed up. When I say 'go,' run over to the wall and swing your butt so the chairs hit it."

"Run?" said Dana. "How are we supposed to run?"

"You know what I mean."

Steve and Dana prepared to move.

"Go!"

Steve and Dana waddled over and swung their chairs toward the wall. They hit only the air. The boys lost their balance, wobbled, and found themselves sitting down again, back-to-back.

"We were early on that one," said Steve.

"Yeah, you think?" said Dana.

They lifted their chair legs off the ground and reset their position.

"Go!"

The boys shuffled and hopped as fast as they could, building up momentum. They didn't want to swing early this time. The wall came sooner than they expected. The sides of their bodies met the side of the boat. The room reverberated with the sound of the impact. Steve and Dana bounced off the wall and ended up sitting down again, back to back.

"Okay. We were a little late that time," said Steve.

"I know," said Dana.

They raised themselves, ready to try again.

"Go!"

This time Steve swung too early, and Dana ran too fast, and the pair toppled to the ground. They skidded headfirst toward the wall, their legs and the chairs' legs flipping into the air. Together they did a great, ugly somersault and came slamming into the floor. The wood splintered and clattered across the ground. Steve and Dana lay on the floor, dazed.

"Beautiful!" Steve said, even though it wasn't.

They rose to their feet, pulled off the ropes, and rubbed their heads.

"High five!" said Dana.

They missed. It was dark.

"Okay," said Dana. "Now, how do we get out?"

Steve reached into his pocket for Grabes's lighter. It was gone. Grabes must have searched him while he was knocked out. His wallet was missing too. The only thing Grabes had left him was his magnifying glass.

That wasn't going to help in the dark.

Steve started walking around again. Here they were, trapped in the hold of a boat at sea, and the only door was twenty-five feet above their head. How could they escape? If this were a Bailey Brothers book, now would be the part where Shawn and Kevin's dad, the famous detective Harris Bailey, would open the hatch and rescue them. Steve shook his head and started groping around in the dark.

He slid his fingertips along the wall and walked the perimeter of the room, hoping to find handholds they could use to climb up. He walked the length of a wall without finding anything. Steve turned and walked until he reached another corner. Still no luck. On the third wall he found a large metal object. Steve gingerly felt it— it was circular, about the size of a car's steering wheel. He brought his hands to his face. They smelled like rust.

Steve didn't have a better plan, so he gripped the wheel with both hands and turned it counterclockwise. The wheel groaned as Steve strained.

There was a hissing. The hissing became a rushing. The rushing echoed off the walls and filled the room. Steve's sneakers felt damp. He looked down, even though he couldn't see anything. His ankles were wet. Now his calves. The room was filling with water.

CHAPTER XXVI

Panic Below Deck!

"WHAT DID YOU DO?" Dana screamed in the dark.

"I don't know!" Steve yelled over the din. "But get ready to swim!"

Before long the water was up to their necks. It came straight from the sea, freezing cold and smelling like fish.

Steve and Dana started swimming. It wouldn't be long till the room was completely filled with water.

"Are we sinking?" yelled Steve.

"No!" screamed Dana. "If we were, water would be coming from the ceiling, too."

"Good!"

"Not good!" said Dana. "We're going to drown!"

"When we get to the ceiling, we have to try to find the hatch," said Steve.

"How will we know when we get to the ceiling?"

"First we'll hit our heads; then we won't be able to breathe."

"Perfect," said Dana. Up and up they went. Steve craned his neck back and took a deep breath. He noticed a faint gold rectangle outlined in the blackness overhead.

"The door!" Steve shouted.

"Where?" asked Dana.

"I'm pointing at it!"

"I can't see your finger!"

"Right!"

Steve swam toward the rectangle. He raised his right hand out of the water to see whether he could touch the ceiling. His hand hit the hatch with a clang. Madly, Steve fumbled above his head, hunting for the valve that would open the hatch. He skinned his knuckles against a protrusion. It was round. He gripped it frantically.

"Dana, over here," Steve yelled.

Steve kept shouting so Dana could follow his voice. Soon he felt his friend's hand on his face. Their heads were now pressed against the roof, and the water was just under their chins.

"The valve is right above our heads!"

Both boys grabbed on to the wheel and twisted it desperately. It moved. The water was up to their foreheads. The boys kept turning the wheel. Steve shut his eyes, now completely underwater. There was a dull groaning. The hatch lifted, and light entered the hold. A rush of water pushed Dana and Steve upward and deposited them on the deck of the ship. They lay on their backs, panting in the fog.

The air was chilly, and the boys were soaked. Water continued to bubble up from the hold and spill across the deck. Steve rolled his head to the left and the right. The ship was long, much longer than Steve had imagined it would be. The deck stretched on and on, interrupted every twenty feet by a hatch like the one they'd just opened. Behind them a tower rose up in the middle of the ship. The tower was crowned by a glass room. Steve discerned the outline of a man slumped in a chair up in the tower. That man was Doug Grabes.

Steve waved his hand to get Dana's attention and pointed at Grabes. Dana's eyes widened. Grabes didn't move. It looked like he was asleep.

"We have to get rid of him," Steve whispered.

"Right," said Dana. "How?"

CHAPTER XXVII

A Treacherous Trap

THE BAILEY BROTHERS' DETECTIVE HANDBOOK has some things to say about traps.

> Shawn and Kevin love a good booby trap. Trapping a crook gives their knuckles a break. You too can trap baddies, just like the Bailey Brothers! Just make like Tarzan and dig a hole in the ground, then cover it with sticks and leaves. Crash! Your unsuspecting suspect will fall right in!

"Well, that's not helpful," said Dana. "There's nowhere to dig."

Steve eyed the hatches. "We don't need to dig."

They walked to the back of the ship, which Steve was pretty sure was called the prow. He and Dana stood looking down at a hatch. "I've got a plan," said Steve. "First we take the door off a hatch on the prow of the ship."

"Don't you mean the stern?" asked Dana.

"Just help me take off this door," said Steve.

They unlocked the hatch. "One, two, three," Dana counted. The boys lifted the steel door at the same time. They stashed it over by a row of bright red buoys.

Dana and Steve peered down into the hold they'd just opened. It was filled three quarters of the way with water.

"Something's moving down there," said Dana.

He was right.

"What is it?" asked Steve.

They got down on their stomachs and peered into the hold. The water was bubbling and swirling. Something was thrashing around wildly. As their eyes adjusted, the boys saw hundreds of tiny pincers breaking the surface of the water.

"Crabs," said Dana. "This must be a fishing boat."

"Perfect," Steve said.

Steve got up and found a bunch of gray tarps over by some huge crab pots. He unfolded a tarp and laid it over the open hold.

"Okay," said Steve. "We're all set. Now for phase two. Let's go wake up Doug Grabes. He's up in the cabin."

"Don't you mean the wheelhouse?" asked Dana.

Steve looked at Dana.

"When did you learn so much about boats?"

Dana shrugged. "I just like books about boats," he said.

Steve shook his head.

Steve and Dana walked up the steps to the wheelhouse. Dana went first. Soon they'd be running back down, and Steve wanted a head start. Dana was much faster than Steve, even when Steve didn't have a sore ankle.

Dana gently opened the door to the wheelhouse. Grabes was snoring loudly. Steve's backpack was lying open on the floor. Grabes had been going through his stuff. Steve's brain boiled with anger.

Furious, Steve pulled out his magnifying glass and threw it at the sleeping man's head. Grabes awoke with a snort.

So that's what magnifying glasses were for.

Doug Grabes was surprised to see the two twelve-year-old boys standing five feet away. Steve and Dana turned and ran.

"Hurry up, Steve!" Dana was right behind him.

Steve was taking the stairs two at a time. He could hear Grabes swearing and breathing and stumbling down after them. Steve jumped down the last four steps and hit the deck hard. He started running toward the stern of the ship. Dana quickly passed him.

"Wait up!" said Steve.

"Hurry up!" said Dana.

"I'll kill you!" said Doug Grabes.

Luckily Grabes's tiny legs made him even slower than Steve. The boys sprinted down the deck till they ran out of ship. They came to their trap, turned, and waited. Grabes jogged down to them and pulled a cruel-looking knife from his pocket. He grinned menacingly.

"It's a boat," said Grabes. "There's nowhere to run."

Steve and Dana stood on one side of the open hold. Grabes stood on the other.

"You go left, I'll go right," said Dana.

Steve nodded. "I'll meet you down at the stern."

"Prow," said Dana.

"Oh no you don't," said Grabes. "I'm not running down this ship again."

Holding his knife in front of him, Doug Grabes took one, two, three strides forward. The third took him onto the tarp, which gave way immediately. Grabes went tumbling down into the hold. The boys heard a

Grabes wielded a cruel-looking knife. . . .

splash, followed quickly by screaming. The crabs must have been pinching.

"I almost feel bad," said Steve. "Almost."

He and Dana picked up the door and put it back on top of the hatch. They sealed it up, then moved some of the pots on top of it, just in case.

Steve and Dana walked back up to the wheelhouse. Steve ran over to his backpack. He pulled out the *Guinness Book of World Records* and opened it. His notebook was safely tucked inside, right next to the torn-out page of symbols from *An Illustrated History of American Quilting*. Grabes hadn't gotten past the secret book-box.

Steve pulled out a pencil and opened up his black notebook.

MYSTERY THREE: WHO KIDNAPPED DANA?   STATUS: SOLVED

SUSPECT	MOTIVE
Doug Grabes	Works for Mr. E
Mr. E.	Wants the book (Grabes had wanted poster— Is Mr. E. a Librarian?)
Rick	Jerk

Steve closed the book with a satisfying snap and put it back in his backpack. He picked his magnifying glass up off the floor and checked it for damage. It looked perfect. Steve slipped it back into his pocket.

On a counter he found his wallet and the silver lighter. He grabbed both, and for the first time he noticed the lighter was engraved.

TO DOUG
FROM M

"Look at this!" Steve said to Dana.

"Yeah," Dana said. "So what?"

"A clue! From M!"

"Who's M?"

"Maybe *M* is for Mackintosh! Maybe Grabes and Mackintosh are in cahoots!"

"Or maybe *M* is for Mom. Also, who says 'cahoots'?"

Steve shook his head. He put the lighter in his backpack.

"All right, Dana," he said. "Can you get us back to shore?"

"Me?"

"You're the boat expert," said Steve.

"I don't know how to drive them."

Steve and Dana looked at the ship's controls. There were hundreds of knobs, dials, and levers. "Maybe we can figure this out," Steve said, staring at a gauge marked AC AMPERES.

Just then a loud horn rattled the windows. Steve's head snapped up in the direction of the sound. Out from the fog came a huge red wall painted with white Chinese characters. Each letter was the size of a house.

"What the heck is that?" asked Steve.

"A freighter," said Dana.

It was coming right toward them.

CHAPTER XXVIII

Shipwreck!

"ABANDON SHIP!" SHOUTED STEVE. He threw on his backpack and followed Dana down the stairs.

The horn sounded again. Steve glanced up. The ship was getting closer. It was headed right toward the middle of their boat.

"Grab a buoy!" shouted Dana. "We'll have a long way to swim."

"Now you're thinking like a sleuth!" said Steve.

They each picked up a red buoy and ran over to the rail of the deck. Steve looked down. It was a long way to the water. Steve and Dana climbed over the railing. The freighter's Klaxon blared. *Here we go again,* thought Steve. He leapt off the edge of the boat.

Steve hit the water with a loud slap. He tasted blood. "I bit my tongue!" he said, whining to no one in particular. Dana was a yard off to his left and already moving furiously away from their boat. Steve gripped his buoy with both hands and started kicking as hard as he could.

He followed Dana, promising himself that he wouldn't look back. A terrible sound, like a ship screaming, came from behind him. Steve broke his promise and turned to look over his shoulder, just in time to see the freighter pierce the middle of their boat. The crab boat split into halves, each of which flew back from the freighter's red hull. In spite of himself Steve was worried for Doug Grabes.

"Man," murmured Dana, who'd turned to watch as well.

The two halves of their boat tipped upward into the air, dipped below the surface, and came bursting back up again. Sea spray erupted in cloudy plumes. Each half of the ship bobbed up and down, but neither sank.

"It's because most of the holds are empty," said Dana. "Filled with air. The wreckage will float for a while."

"All right, I get it," Steve said. "You know a lot about boatth."

"Why are you talking funny?" Dana asked.

"I bit my tongue. Really hard."

Dana started laughing. "You sound like that old librarian. What was his name? Mr. Beckley. 'Thilenth, pleathe!'"

"Mithter Beckley wath a national hero," Steve said fiercely.

"Okay," said Dana.

They watched in silence.

"Do you think Grabeth ith all right?" Steve asked.

"Should be," said Dana. "Except for the crabs."

Up on the deck of the freighter Steve could make out the outlines of men running around and gesticulating wildly.

"Let'th get out of here," said Steve.

Dana nodded toward the sun, which broke faintly through the fog. "That's east. Land should be that way."

Dana and Steve started kicking toward the shore. Steve hoped land was close.

"Are you sure thith ith the way back to Ocean Park?" he shouted up to Dana.

"No," said Dana without looking back.

CHAPTER XXIX

An Unfortunate Deadline

AN HOUR LATER STEVE AND DANA washed up on the beach. The swim back had been exhausting. They didn't even know whether they were heading in the right direction until a Coast Guard cutter passed them, heading toward the shipwreck.

Now Steve was curled up in the sand. His tongue was still killing him. He felt like taking a nap.

Seagulls circled and squawked overhead. Their screeching was interrupted by the ringing of the Ocean Park clock tower. It was seven in the morning.

"We have school today," said Dana, who'd collapsed next to Steve.

"Yeah," said Steve. "And our reportth are due."

Dana groaned. "I didn't do any work on mine."

"Well, now I know a bunch about quiltth," said Steve. "And you know a bunch about detective work."

They stared at the birds.

"Okay," said Steve, "I've got a plan. Let'th go thee Mith Gilfeather. We can get her to give uth more time on the reportth. Then we can thpend the retht of the day thleuthing."

"I'm done sleuthing," Dana said.

"But we've got a mythtery to tholve," said Steve.

"I'm going to go home, take a shower, and see if my mom will let me take the day off to go to the library and start my report."

"Okay," said Steve, even though it didn't feel okay at all.

They stood up and walked in opposite directions.

Steve got to Ocean Park Middle School at seven thirty a.m. The parking lot was deserted. He sat under a tree by the athletic field, where he was out of sight from the street but could see the school's front entrance. He didn't know what time Ms. Gilfeather got to school, but he was ready to wait. There was no need. Five minutes after Steve sat down, his social studies teacher came biking up the road, her ponytail bouncing behind her.

Steve picked himself up and met her in the parking lot. She looked surprised to see him but smiled pleasantly.

"Good morning, Steve," she said. "How was your weekend?"

"Good quethtion," said Steve.

"Are you okay? You're talking funny."

"I bit my tongue," said Steve.

"And you're dressed like a sailor."

"It'th a dithguise."

Ms. Gilfeather raised her eyebrows.

"Can I talk to you for a minute?" Steve asked.

"Of course." Ms Gilfeather took out her keys and opened the front door to the school. Steve followed her inside, and she locked the door behind them. The sound of their footsteps bounced around the halls. It was weird to see the school empty.

Ms. Gilfeather opened up her classroom and flipped a switch. The lights hummed. She put her tote bag on her chair and sat on the edge of her desk. Steve took a seat at a desk.

"What's wrong, Steve?"

Steve hesitated. "Remember when you thaid I might find needlework more interethting than I thought?"

She nodded.

"Well, you were right."

Ms. Gilfeather beamed. "That's fantastic, Steve!"

"But I don't have my report done," he said.

Ms. Gilfeather frowned. "Why not?"

"Well," said Steve. "The government thinkth that I'm a private detective and a national traitor, and I thpent the weekend running from the polithe and being held captive on a fishing boat."

Ms. Gilfeather smiled patiently and said, "Steve, that is the single worst excuse for not doing your homework that I have ever heard."

Steve was crushed. "I'm therious, Mith Gilfeather!"

"So you're telling me that you don't have any work done?"

"I'm a fugitive from the law!"

"Steve."

Steve couldn't get an F on this paper. It was time to switch tactics. He pulled out his secret book-box, opened it, and pulled out his black notebook. It was still damp. "Well," he said. "I have done a bunch of rethearch on quiltth."

Ms. Gilfeather studied the notebook skeptically. "What's all this?" she asked, pointing to the list of quilting symbols.

"Thothe are common quilting thymbolth," he said.

"Thimbles?" said Ms. Gilfeather.

"Thymbolth," Steve said.

"Oh, symbols."

"Yeah, and look here," Steve said turning a soggy page. "Thith ith all about the Maguffin Quilt. The generalth uthed quiltth to communicate during the American Revolution." Steve delicately turned a soggy page.

Ms. Gilfeather looked up and sighed. "All right, Steve. I can see you've done some research. I'll tell you what. I'll give you partial credit for your notes."

"Okay," he said.

"But I still don't believe your story."

"Okay."

Ms. Gilfeather put his notebook in her drawer.

"Wait," said Steve. "I need that. Can't you make a photocopy?"

Ms. Gilfeather sighed. "Come on," she said.

They walked down to the school office.

Out of nowhere, they heard the sound of heavy shoes clacking against the floor.

Someone else was here. The footsteps were uneven—the person was walking with a limp.

"I thought we were the only ones at school," said Steve.

"Me too," said Ms. Gilfeather.

Steve braced, ready to bolt.

First there was a shadow. Then a figure rounded the corner.

Oh, my! It's Joe!

CHAPTER XXX

The Figure Revealed

IT WAS THE JANITOR, JOE.

"Morning, Mary," said the janitor.

"Good morning, Joe."

Steve put his hand up to his face so Joe couldn't recognize him.

"Morning, Steve," said Joe.

"Good morning."

They passed by Joe and entered the office. Ms. Gilfeather pressed some buttons on the copier and it whirred into life. Steve rummaged through the lost-and-found box and found a red hooded sweatshirt. He put it on over his sailor shirt and pulled the hood tight over his head. It wasn't a great disguise, but it would do. He'd return it tomorrow.

Ms. Gilfeather handed Steve's notebook back to him. He opened up his book-box and put the notebook in the secret compartment.

"That's a nifty place to store things. What is it?"

"My thecret book-box. I made it mythelf."

"A hollow book." Ms. Gilfeather picked it up and looked at it. She handed it back to Steve. "What a great hiding place."

"Yeah," Steve said dejectedly.

"Where'd you learn that trick?"

"The *Bailey Brotherth' Detective Handbook*."

"Very cool, Steve." Ms. Gilfeather wrinkled her nose, which she did when she was about to make a joke. "Too bad you didn't pick detectives for your essay topic."

"You're telling me," Steve said. He walked toward the door. "Mith Gilfeather, I won't be in clath today."

"Why not?"

"I have a mythtery to tholve." Steve shut the door behind him. It was a good sentence to end with, but it would have sounded better if Steve hadn't bitten his tongue. Steve walked down the hall and slipped out the rear entrance of the school.

Ocean Park stretched before him, but his case was at a dead end.

CHAPTER XXXI

A Startling Realization

THE BAILEY BROTHERS' DETECTIVE HANDBOOK says that if you're stuck on a case, you should treat yourself to an ice cream. Shawn Bailey's favorite flavor was chocolate. Kevin liked vanilla. Steve was partial to mint chip, but he didn't think that flavor was around back when the Bailey Brothers were solving their cases.

Steve was waiting outside Rocky's Ice Creamery when it opened at ten a.m. He took his hood off so the guy working there wouldn't think he was going to rob the place.

"One mint chip cone, pleathe," Steve said.

The man behind the counter looked at Steve strangely.

"I bit my tongue," said Steve. "In a shipwreck."

He took out his wallet and handed over his last five dollars. The ice cream felt cool and soothing against his tongue. Steve sat in a booth in the corner and pulled out his secret book-box. Then he opened up his notebook and put it on the table.

He thought of Beckley's last words: "Look in the book. Use a symbol."

Steve took out Beckley's list of symbols and studied it, just in case he had missed anything. He looked at the page with his magnifying glass. Maybe Mr. Beckley had written secret instructions in tiny handwriting. Nope.

Steve wadded up the page and held it in a tight fist.

He started pacing in the back of the ice cream parlor.

His brain gave him nothing.

Well, this was it. He gave up. At this point he might as well turn himself in and hope the Librarians showed him some mercy. Or maybe he could skip town—catch a bus to South Dakota and live on a cattle ranch.

Why did he think he could solve this case? He wasn't a detective. He was just a kid with a magnifying glass who read mysteries and hid his stuff in a hollowed-out book.

He raised his ice cream cone to his mouth. He missed.

That was it.

Steve knew where Mr. Beckley had hidden the quilt.

CHAPTER XXXII

Unexpected Assistance

STEVE STOOD UP AND HEADED FOR THE EXIT. But when he got to the door, he froze. A black and white police cruiser was parked right outside the ice cream parlor. Rick Elliot sat in the driver's seat.

Steve hoped Rick wouldn't look up and see him.

Rick looked up and saw him.

For a second neither of them moved. Then Rick got out of the car. His hand was on his pistol.

Steve inhaled and walked out of the door.

"Hi there, Rick," said Steve.

"A lot of people are looking for you, young man."

"Rick," said Steve, "I'm not guilty of treason." The s in treason came out smoothly—Steve's tongue was feeling better, thanks to the ice cream.

Rick smiled. "Well, Steve, I didn't ever really think you were. See, I can read people. And no offense, but you don't exactly seem like a criminal mastermind. Chief Clumber, on the other hand—he thinks you're a pretty dangerous man."

"So do a lot of people."

"Tell you what, Steve. Why don't you come to the station and we can sort this out?"

"I can't, Rick. I'm innocent, but I can't prove it right now." Steve hated to do it, but he needed to ask Rick for a favor. "Can you take me to the Ocean Park Public Library?"

Rick tugged on his mustache.

"All right, Steve," he said. "Hop in the car."

"Thanks!" Steve ran over to Rick's police car.

"Not in the back, Steve. That's where we put the criminals. Get in the front."

Steve laughed and hopped in the front seat. Rick came over and leaned in the window. "Now, I've got to call in to the station and make up a cover story for us. I know—I'll tell them I'm going to take an ice cream break."

"Okay," said Steve, smiling. Rick walked back toward the ice cream parlor.

"Hey, Rick," Steve said. Rick stopped and turned around. "I'm not a detective, either."

Rick smiled. "I know."

Maybe Rick wasn't such a jerk after all.

Rick walked down the block and with his back to Steve, started talking into his shoulder.

To Steve's surprise Rick's voice came faintly from a speaker in the dashboard. The car's police radio was on. Steve reached for a knob and turned up the volume.

"Repeat: Elliot to base, Elliot to base. Over."

"Base to Elliot. What's your situation?" replied a gruff voice.

"Tell Clumber I've picked up the detective. I'm bringing him in to the station."

Steve's eyes widened.

"Roger that. Proceed with caution—he could be dangerous."

Rick looked over his shoulder and grinned at Steve. Steve smiled weakly and waved. Rick turned back around.

"Don't worry about me," Rick said. "He thinks I'm on his side. He's sitting in my squad car waiting for me to give him a ride to the library."

Rick laughed.

Rick was an idiot.

And a jerk.

Steve had to get out of there.

CHAPTER XXXIII

High Octane!

DESPITE THE FACT THAT Shawn and Kevin Bailey own a lightning-fast roadster named the Jalopy, despite the fact that every single one of the Bailey Brothers Mysteries has the brothers chasing criminals at top speeds, racing up mountain roads or around dangerous cliffs—despite all this, The Bailey Brothers' Detective Handbook has no advice on how to drive a car. The thing is, you don't have to be a sleuth to drive a car. You just have to be sixteen years old.

Steve wasn't sixteen, but he was desperate. He slid over to the driver's side. Rick's keys were in the ignition. He turned them hard, and the engine roared to life. Rick spun around. He saw Steve behind the wheel and turned white.

Steve tried to think of what his mom did when she drove. He adjusted the rearview mirror. Rick was running back to the car. Steve fastened his seat belt. He moved the gearshift to D. The car jolted into life. Rick was only a few feet away. Steve locked the doors. He grabbed the steering wheel and slid his feet down to reach the pedals. He pressed the one on the left. Nothing happened. He pressed the one on the right. The car leapt forward. Steve cut the wheel to the left but still ended up clipping the bumper of a car parked in front of him. There was a crunching sound and the car made a small jump. Steve was on the road.

"He stole my car!" came Rick's voice through the speaker. "The detective stole my car!" There was the sound of a shuffle. "Stop!" said Rick. "Police! I need to commandeer your bicycle." Steve laughed and turned the volume down on the police radio.

It was hard to see over the wheel and keep his foot on the pedal at the same time. The car lurched forward every time Steve hit the gas, then slowed when Steve peeked over the wheel.

Steve made a left off Main Street onto Beachfront Drive. The ocean stretched out on his left, gleaming in the late morning sun. The library was about two miles away. Steve rolled down his window and steered with one hand. This driving was pretty great.

Then he heard a siren. He looked over his shoulder and saw a squad car pull onto the road behind him. Its lights flashed frantically.

"Pull over!" came a stern voice over a bullhorn.

Steve put both hands on the wheel and pressed down hard on the gas. He couldn't really see where he was driving, but he was driving really fast. Another siren rang out. Steve turned around and saw a hulking white bus. The bookmobile.

This was getting interesting.

Steve felt like some chase music. He flipped on the stereo.

Smooth jazz.

Of course Rick listened to smooth jazz.

It had been a while since Steve had checked the road, so he eased off the gas and looked up. He was shocked to discover that the front of his car was four inches from the back of a green sedan. Steve slipped back down and slammed on the brake. He heard the squad car screeching behind him. Steve sped up again.

This wasn't working. Steve needed to be able to go fast and see where he was going at the same time. He groped around the passenger seat, grabbed his backpack, and jammed it onto the gas pedal. The car lurched forward. Steve got up on his knees. This was better.

Steve's police car was coming up fast on the green sedan. He cut the wheel to the left and veered into the other lane. His pursuers did the same. All three vehicles passed the green sedan and swerved back in front of it.

Faster and faster they went. Steve figured it would be good to turn on his siren. He flipped a button on the dash that had a picture of sound waves. The siren pierced the air.

"This is Chief Frank Clumber of the Ocean Park Police Department," a voice blared from behind. "Pull over now, detective!"

"This is Agent Mackintosh!" cried another voice. "Give up, Steven!"

Steve grabbed a receiver off the dash. "My name is Steve!" he shouted into it.

Steve's turn was approaching on the right. He spun the steering wheel around, and his tires squealed. He could still hear the police behind him. The library was just a block away.

"Pull over!" came a voice from Steve's left. He turned and saw Chief Clumber driving alongside him. Clumber looked furious. Steve looked ahead.

The library was on the right. For the first time Steve realized that his backpack was covering up the brake pedal. That was going to make it hard to stop.

Steve yanked on the emergency brake. He turned the wheel to the right. Clumber's car shot ahead, followed by the bookmobile. Steve's car spun off to the right, jacked up onto the curb, and came skidding to a stop on the library's front lawn. He grabbed his backpack, opened his door, and ran up the library's path.

Clumber's cruiser pulled up in front of the building.

Ms. Bundt ran out of the library's front entrance. Dana came out behind her, holding a book about detectives.

Mackintosh came loping up the street. He was overtaken by Rick, who was riding a powder-blue bicycle with a basket on the front. Ms. Gilfeather followed on foot behind him. She was shouting.

Steve climbed up on the bronze book sculpture and rubbed it for good luck. He threw his hands in the air.

"Everyone!" he said. "I've solved the mystery!"

CHAPTER XXXIV

A Mystery Revealed

THE BAILEY BROTHERS' DETECTIVE HANDBOOK has some advice about bringing your case to a close:

> Shawn and Kevin think the neatest way to solve a mystery is to do it in front of everyone they know! When they reach a solution, they invite everyone involved in a case to come hear it. It's fun to watch the surprised looks on their faces—it's the acest way to end a case!

Steve looked across the lawn. He hadn't needed to invite everybody. They'd shown up on their own. Rick, Chief Clumber, Dana, Mackintosh, Ms. Bundt, and Ms. Gilfeather gathered in front of the statue.

"What's going on here?" Chief Clumber asked, a pair of handcuffs in his hand. Mackintosh walked over to the chief and showed him his badge.

"I'm Special Agent Mackintosh," he said. "Good to meet you in person, Chief. Steve here has been working on a case of some interest to the United States government. We'd like to hear what he has to say."

Chief Clumber put his handcuffs away.

Mackintosh smiled at Steve. "Please, Steve. Go ahead."

Steve climbed up on the sculpture for dramatic effect. He cleared his throat and began. "As most of you know, two days ago I was approached by some . . ." Steve didn't feel at liberty to divulge the role of the United States Library. "By some government agents working undercover as librarians."

Mackintosh and Ms. Bundt smiled gratefully.

"Librarians!" Rick said, cackling.

"Yes," said Steve. "Librarians. They thought I might be able to help them track down a missing quilt."

"A quilt?" asked Rick.

"Yes, a very important quilt," said Steve. "Please, Rick, try to follow along."

Rick snorted but didn't say anything.

"We only had one clue: Mr. Beckley, the only man who knew the quilt's whereabouts, told Ms. Bundt to look in a book." Steve opened his backpack and pulled out *An Illustrated History of American Quilting*. "This is Mr. Beckley's book. I checked it out from the library on Saturday. Since then, a lot of people have tried to get their hands on it, which is interesting. Because this book is completely useless." Steve threw the book on the grass. Ms. Bundt and Mackintosh gasped. Ms. Bundt picked up the book and brushed some mud from its cover.

"What are you talking about, Steven?" said Mackintosh. "Beckley said to look in the book."

"Sure he did," said Steve. "But this isn't the book he meant. You were looking for a book that held a clue. You should have been looking for a book that held the quilt." Steve crouched down and rapped the bronze sculpture with his hands. It made a hollow ringing sound. "A secret book-box."

Ms. Bundt gasped.

"Ladies and gentlemen, the quilt is inside this book!"

"But how do we get it open?" asked Mackintosh.

Steve peered at the sculpture, running his hands

Steve stood on the sculpture, the breeze blowing
back his hair, looking completely ace.

across its surface. He found a small depression about the size of his thumb.

"It's simple. Just like Beckley told Ms. Bundt: Use a thimble."

"You mean a symbol," said Ms. Bundt.

"He bit his tongue," explained Dana. "He's been talking like that all morning."

"No," said Steve. "I mean a thimble. Mr. Beckley had a lisp, right?"

Ms. Bundt nodded.

"So when he said thimble, Ms. Bundt, you assumed he meant a symbol. But a thimble is actually the key."

"Brilliant," Ms. Bundt said to herself.

"Well, does anybody have a thimble?" asked Chief Clumber.

"I do," said Rick, and pulled a thimble out of his pocket. Everyone stared. "What?" said Rick. "I like needlepoint. It's relaxing."

Rick handed the thimble up to Steve. Steve put it on his thumb, and put his thumb into the groove on the sculpture. It fit snugly. He turned his hand, and something inside the book clicked.

Steve grabbed the edge of the bronze sculpture as if he were going to open the cover. A metal panel swung loose.

"Ladies and gentlemen," said Steve, "I give you the Maguffin Quilt."

Steve lifted the panel and revealed a secret compartment. Everyone gathered around to look inside.

The book-box was empty.

CHAPTER XXXV

Mr. E.

S<small>TEVE DEFLATED</small>.

Mackintosh looked at the sky.

Ms. Bundt put her head in her hands.

"Mr. E. got here first," she said. "Disaster."

Chief Clumber spoke up. "What does this Mr. E. look like? We'll put a bulletin out. He won't make it out of the county."

Mackintosh shook his head. "Nobody knows what he looks like. No one's ever seen him."

Rick straightened up. "I'll track him down. I'll start by dusting this sculpture for fingerprints. Don't worry. Rick Elliot always gets his man."

Steve was walking in a circle on the lawn. His head snapped up. "Wait. I'm not sure Mr. E. is a man."

Rick gave an exasperated yelp. "Really, Steve? You think he's a bird?"

"No," said Steve. "I think he's a she. And she's right here." Steve straightened up. "Mr. E. is Ms. Gilfeather!"

All eyes turned toward Steve's teacher. Ms. Gilfeather was shocked. "Me?" she said. "What are you talking about?"

"You set me up, Ms. Gilfeather. I was a patsy."

"Steve, this is crazy."

Steve kept circling, walking faster and faster. His brain started untangling the solution. "You needed to get your hands on *An Illustrated History of American Quilting*. But you knew the book was being watched. So you had your henchman, Doug Grabes, leave his card for the person who did check it out. And then you assigned a report on early American needlework."

The crowd looked skeptical.

"It's the perfect cover, right? Nobody would expect a kid to be part of a plot to sell America's secrets. It's ridiculous."

Mackintosh and Ms. Bundt were shamefaced.

Steve continued. "But things went wrong. I got picked up by the Librarians and barely escaped. When I wouldn't give the page of symbols to Grabes, you had him kidnap me and Dana. But we escaped. Which is why, when I showed up at your classroom this morning, you wanted my notes."

Steve paused to let his mouth catch up to his mind. "Of course, you figured out that Beckley's book was worthless before I did. In the office you saw my bookbox and you had heard me say 'thimble.' So you came over early this morning and took the quilt."

"I don't know what you're talking about, Steve," said Ms. Gilfeather.

"And how about this?" Steve pulled the lighter out of his backpack and tossed it to Ms. Gilfeather. She caught it with one hand.

"What's this?" she asked.

"It's Doug Grabes's lighter, engraved from M. Your name is Mary. I heard Joe call you that this morning."

"Lots of people have names that start with M, Steve," said Ms. Gilfeather. "Maybe M is for Mom."

Dana smirked.

"Then let me ask you this. Rick commandeered your bike in front of Rocky's Ice Creamery. Why were you riding your bike on the east side of town at ten in the morning? Shouldn't you have been in class?"

"I was feeling sick."

"Or you were skipping town," said Steve. "In fact,

I'll bet the only reason you're still here at the library is that Rick is sitting on your bike."

Everyone looked at Rick. He was uncomfortable with the sudden attention.

"Rick," said Steve, "look in that basket."

"Oh, come on," said Ms. Gilfeather. "Is anyone really going to listen to him? He's just a kid."

Steve's head whipped around, and he looked at his teacher defiantly.

"I'm not just a kid, Ms. Gilfeather. I'm a detective."

As soon as the sentence came out of Steve's mouth, he repeated it a couple times in his head. It sounded right.

Rick looked at Chief Clumber. The chief nodded.

Rick reached into the bike's basket and pulled out Ms. Gilfeather's tote bag. He turned the bag upside down and gave it a shake. Out plopped a white quilt, folded into a neat square.

"The Maguffin Quilt!" cried Ms. Bundt. She immediately snatched it up and disappeared into the library.

"You've got the right to remain silent," said Mackintosh, taking out a pair of handcuffs.

Ms. Gilfeather glowered at Steve.

"Why'd you do it?" Steve asked.

"Why do you think?" said Ms. Gilfeather. "For the money. You expect me to live on a teacher's salary?"

Dana looked astonished. "I didn't know you were an international criminal, Ms. Gilfeather."

Ms. Gilfeather smiled sweetly. "There are a lot of things kids don't know about their teachers."

Mackintosh led Ms. Gilfeather into the library.

Steve looked at Rick and grinned. "Lucky you picked up that bike," he said.

Rick beamed. "Does this mean I solved the case?"

Chief Clumber put his hand on Rick's shoulder and smiled warmly. "No," he said.

CHAPTER XXXVI

An Ace Detective

STEVE RODE IN THE PASSENGER SEAT of the bookmobile. Ms. Bundt drove. Dana was in the back, reading a book about boats.

"So you're in charge of the quilt now, huh?" Steve asked.

"Yes," said Ms. Bundt. "But we have a lot less to worry about with Ms. Gilfeather out of the way."

"And Doug Grabes?"

"The Coast Guard picked him up this morning. Now he's in Librarian custody."

The bookmobile pulled in front of Steve's house. He gave a sigh of relief.

Ms. Bundt turned off the engine. "So what about you, Steve?" she asked. "Summer's coming. You could work in the library. We could use someone like you."

"No thanks," said Steve. "I think I'm going to open a business. The Brixton Brothers Detective Agency."

Ms. Bundt looked confused. "I didn't know you had a brother," said Ms. Bundt.

"I don't," said Steve. "It just sounds better."

Ms. Bundt nodded, unconvinced.

Steve whipped around in his chair. "Hey, Dana!" he said excitedly. "How would you like it if I called you my brother?"

Dana looked up from his book and groaned. "I'd rather you call me chum."

Steve turned back around. "Well, I'm still naming it that."

"Detecting is tough work," said Ms. Bundt. "If there's ever anything we Librarians can do for you, let me know. Of course, I have to ask that you keep the nature of the Library secret. The knowledge of who we are can't extend past you, Dana, and Chief Clumber."

"Sure," said Steve.

"Right," said Dana.

Steve reached for the handle on the passenger door.

"Not so fast," said Ms. Bundt. She reached into her handbag and pulled out a flimsy sheet of yellow paper.

Steve read:

PATRON:
Steve Brixton

DAMAGE TO

*An Illustrated History
of Early American Quilting:*

- Missing page (pp. 47–48)
- Severe water damage
- Mud and grass stains

FINE ASSESSMENT:
$2,000,000.00

Steve's vision went blurry briefly. "For a book?" he asked.

"It's damaged beyond repair, Steve," said Ms. Bundt severely. "That book was priceless."

"Well, you didn't seem to have any trouble coming

up with a price here," said Steve, staring at those zeroes.

Ms. Bundt smiled, took the paper from Steve's hand, and tore it in two. "The Librarians will forgive your fines," said Ms. Bundt, "as a thank-you for your work."

Steve breathed for what felt like the first time in a minute.

"And there's this," said Ms. Bundt, reaching into her purse again. She pulled out three bills and some change. "Three dollars and forty-five cents. The overdue fines you paid in the limo. Mackintosh asked me to return it with his gratitude."

"Thanks," said Steve, looking at the money in his hand, "but I gave him a five-dollar bill."

"Don't press your luck, Steve," said Ms. Bundt.

"Right." Steve climbed down from the bus. The bookmobile pulled away. Steve stood in front of his house and felt the ocean breeze on his face. Then, abruptly, his front door swung open and Carol Brixton came rushing down to the sidewalk. When she got to Steve, she paused, looked him up and down, and hugged him.

"Steve!" she said. "What is going on? I got your note and I've been worried to death. Rick said you ran away from a police station."

"Mom, I solved my first real case. I'm a detective."

"I know," said Carol Brixton. "You're all over the television."

"Really?" said Steve. They started walking up the path to his house. "I wonder what my next case will be."

"I know," said his mom. "The Mystery of Taking the Garbage Out."

"I mean my next *real* case."

That, of course, would be *The Ghostwriter Secret*. But that's a whole other mystery.

Sunday

IT WAS SUNDAY, which was Steve Brixton's least favorite day of the week, and the sun was setting, which was Steve Brixton's least favorite part of a Sunday. But Steve was on his living room couch reading Bailey Brothers #19: *The Strange Case of the Strangest Stranger*, which was part of Steve Brixton's most favorite series of all time: the Bailey Brothers Mysteries.

The Bailey Brothers Mysteries were fifty-eight high-octane adventures featuring Shawn and Kevin Bailey, two quick-thinking, hard-punching teens who never met a case they couldn't crack, a motorcycle they couldn't ride, or an avalanche they couldn't cause and subsequently survive. Sleuthing ran in their family: They were the sons of the great American detective

Harris Bailey, and they were terrific sleuths in their own right.

There were fifty-eight thrilling and perfect Bailey Brothers mysteries in all—starting with Bailey Brothers #1: *The Treasure in Trouble Harbor* and ending with Bailey Brothers #58: *Spacejacked!*—all written by the same author, MacArthur Bart.

MacArthur Bart, a.k.a. America's Mystery King, a.k.a. Steve's hero, had also written the book Steve loved above all others: *The Bailey Brothers' Detective Handbook*. The handbook was packed with Real Crime-Solving Tips—stuff like How to Make a Plaster Cast of a Scoundrel's Shoe Print and Foolproof Methods for Defusing Some Kinds of Time Bombs. Basically all the high-level supersleuth stuff.

Steve had the handbook pretty much memorized, but he still carried it around with him wherever he went. In fact Steve had all the plots to the Bailey Brothers Mysteries memorized, but he still liked reading the books second and third times. Plus it was research, since a few weeks ago Steve had officially opened his own business, the Brixton Brothers Detective Agency. Steve didn't have a brother, or even a sister, but putting "brothers" in the name of your detective agency was a surefire way to make it sound totally ace.

Right now Steve didn't have a case to work on, which was why he was lying on the couch—the living room aglow with the last of the day's sun—and finishing chapter eighteen of his book. A gang of car thieves had just captured the Bailey Brothers and was holding the boys in a sea-cave hideout:

"You creeps will never get away with this!" dark-haired Shawn Bailey hollered. "Crime doesn't pay!"

The large lawbreaker with the salt-and-pepper beard looked up from the game of cards. "It doesn't, eh?" he growled. "Then hows come we've got enough tourin' cars and roadsters stashed away in the old barn to make a fortune?"

Shawn and Kevin exchanged a knowing glance. Now they knew where the lawbreakers were stowing the stolen cars! If only they could get free and notify the police. Behind their backs the brothers redoubled their efforts to undo the knots that bound their hands.

"Gin!" shouted the tattooed crook, slapping his cards on the table. "I win again!"

The bearded hood turned to his fellow criminal and frowned. "Go sit on a stalactite, Charlie."

"I think you mean stalagmite," interrupted Kevin, who had taken honors in geology. "Stalactites grow from the roof, and stalagmites grow from the ground."

"An easy way to remember," Shawn chimed in, "is that the c in 'stalactite' stands for 'ceiling,' and the g in 'stalagmite' stands for 'ground.'"

"Enough!" roared the bearded lowlife. "I'm gettin' tired of all this jabberin'. Charlie, gag this pair of Goody Two-shoes until Smokestacks Samuels gets back and tells us what to do with them."

The man called Charlie stood up and grinned. Gripping two oily rags in his tattooed hand, he limped over to the corner of the cavern where Shawn and Kevin were kept. "This ought to muffle youse two." He sauntered up to Shawn first and reached for the boy's face.

Just then, Shawn untied the last knot and freed his hands. Quickly, he brought his fist around in a powerful haymaker punch to Charlie's solar plexus! The goon collapsed on the limestone floor.

"You kayoed him, Shawn!" whooped Kevin. "Coach Biltmore would be proud!"

Shawn grinned and removed the knife from Charlie's belt. He hurried over to his brother, making sure to hold the knife with its blade pointing down while he ran, and quickly sawed through Kevin's bonds.

Meanwhile the big bearded baddie was lumbering toward them, holding a blackjack in his left hand. "It's gonna be fun whackin' you two over the head," he snarled.

"One, two, three!" counted Kevin, and at once the two brothers bum-rushed their opponent. The large man flew back against the cavern wall and slumped to the floor, unconscious.

"Jumping junipers!" Kevin exclaimed, brushing his blond hair aside. "We sure took care of those two!"

"You bet we did," his younger brother replied. "Now what do you say we tie them up and hide out in this cave? I'll bet you dollars to doorknobs Smokestacks Samuels will be back any minute."

"We can surprise him!" Shawn agreed. "Then we'll learn his real identity!"

"I can't wait to find out who the ringleader of the Viper Gang really is," Kevin remarked.

Suddenly a silhouette appeared on the rocky outcrop near the roof of the cavern. A high, clear voice rang out in the darkness. "You boys will never make it out of here alive. Nobody messes with Smokestacks Samuels!"

Just then, a high, clear voice rang out in the Brixton household. Steve froze.

MYSTERY. ADVENTURE. HOMEWORK.

ENTER THE WORLD OF DAN GUTMAN.

PUBLISHED BY SIMON & SCHUSTER
BOOKS FOR YOUNG READERS
KIDS.SIMONANDSCHUSTER.COM

Just because you're
a kid, it doesn't
mean you can't
solve crimes.

But it probably
means you won't
solve them well.

Did you **LOVE** this book?

Want to get access to great books for **FREE?**

Join